ONLY HUMAN

Copyright 2018 by Stephen Wylie

First published in Great Britain in 2018 by Stephen Wylie

Paperback edition published in 2018

All rights reserved. No part of this publication may be reproduced, stored in a retrieval system, or transmitted, in any form or by any means without the prior permission of the publisher, nor be otherwise circulated in any form of binding or cover other than that in which it is published and without similar condition being imposed on the subsequent purchaser.

All characters in this publication are fictitious and any resemblance to real persons, living or dead is purely coincidental.

Cover designed by Stephen Wylie and featuring Stephen Wylie. Front and back photographs taken and edited by Stephen Wylie

ISBN 978 0 244 08805 7

Acknowledgements & A Few Words

Thank you to Rachel for giving me the faith and belief to finish this project. I am grateful to her for following the story wherever it led, however dark, giving me the confidence to continue and for giving me the strength to go on when I didn't think I could.

There are no page numbers in this book because a man's memories and existence cannot be numbered or put in order. They all follow and interact with each other making them the man in front of you. Labeling them with a number just seemed wrong and insensitive given those very same feelings play such a big part in the decline of a once proud individual, a man who loved, had a glimpse of happiness and tasted contentment.

There will be mistakes in this book that you spot, of that I am sure. I don't apologise for this, instead I point to that fact that everything with this book was done by me. In keeping with the theme, I wrote it completely alone…..

People ask me where the idea and inspiration for this book came from. "Is it you?" they ask. I really have no idea is the true answer. What you're about to read came to me like nothing else I have ever known. Some moments from my past yes. Distorted, twisted and taken completely out of context, but others I literally let develop as they unearthed themselves. I had no idea where the story was going next, or who would be introduced into it. I simply documented the journey. Like an explorer writing a map for others, I hope you enjoy following in my footsteps.

"There is a dark room somewhere in our subconscious. A room that is so shut off, lurking down a long and sinister corridor which lets in no light. No light and no warmth. Nothing can grow there, nothing positive abides there, nothing can live and prosper. Nothing of any good anyway….."

The Bull is always watching, but so too are the ones you love.

ENJOY YOUR LIFE
MAKE THE RIGHT CHOICES
AND BE CAREFUL.

THE BULL IS ALWAYS WATCHING

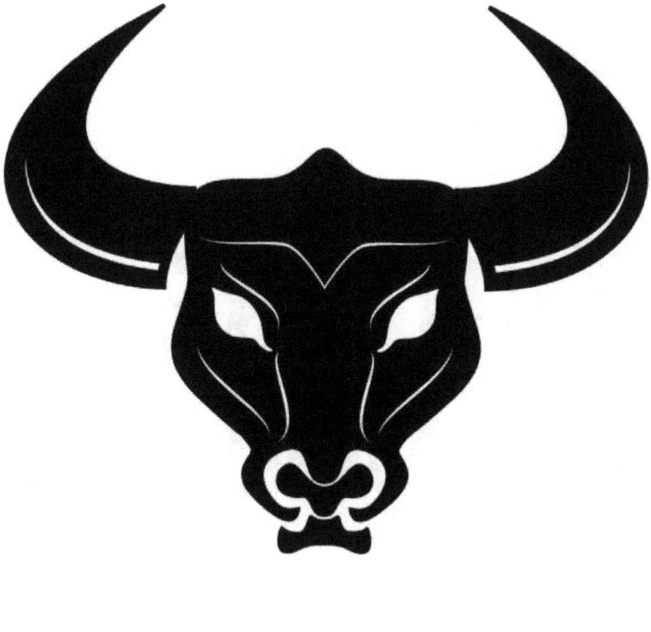

YOU ARE ALONE

ONLY HUMAN

Home
Childhood
Education
Bogey Man
Confidence
Virginity
Adolescence
Knocked Senseless
Love Song
Winter
Anger
Two Lovers
Taxi For One
Losing It
Insomnia
Beelzebub
Loneliness
Merry Christmas
Happy New Year
January
Fog
The Deep Blue Sea
Solo, Solitude and Soul
Depression

HOME

You open your eyes; Sun pours through the bay window spreading light, happiness and hope across the room. Birds sing to welcome a new day, chirpy happy songs of love and excitement. In the distance, you can hear a tractor setting off on its daily chores, it'll be at least twelve hours before you hear that same tractor making the return journey. You briefly close your eyes and for a second you are sure you can smell the diesel fumes from its rustic exhaust as they spread like a bank of fog across the lush and green fields that separate you and the vehicle spewing them out.

Morning has broken and with it brings the sharp but exciting reminder of everything that is your life. Her, home, bliss, blessed, a life that is charmed and beyond your wildest dreams.

You can hear the ruffle of cotton just outside the perfect world inside your ears as you turn your head to your right, gentle and fresh, it smells the way it did when you brought it in off the washing line the day before. Summer breeze with a complimentary mix of natural flowers and pollen, blown around at natures content. Lying in its incredible scent makes you feel like one of those families of an advert for Lenor! Only your rest is real, this is the way you wake every morning and the way you want to wake up every day for the rest of your life.

You turn your head fully and look at the angelic presence that shares your bed this morning and every morning. The most glorious sunrise saved just for you when you open your eyes. Resting her head on an equally inviting pillow is the woman you love. The woman you would die for, the woman you want to be with forever. Your eternal amour, your absolute everything.

Her eyes are closed, but it doesn't stop the fascination and adoration. You gaze straight into her sleepy eyes as you prop yourself up on your elbows and turn to your right to get a closer look. She is gorgeous, beautiful in mind, body and soul. You are lucky she let you this close, lucky she let you in. Extremely grateful, you are the luckiest man alive.

You move forward slowly, determined not to wake her from her slumber, then kiss her gently on the forehead. Your lips are amazed at how soft her skin feels and how fresh she smells, like a hundred flowers in the springtime, her skin has a glow to match. You are seeing nature at its most beautiful best, perfection and

completeness, lying here next to her makes everything outside slip away.
Your cockerel crows and shatters the moment, making you chuckle out loud at the thought of such a brash and primitive creature being able to smash the ambience of such a beautiful moment, a special and serene thirty seconds that only you were privy to. A vision of sheer beauty and love that you will 'snapshot' in your mind forever. You raise your index fingers and thumbs to the air to make a square. Frame that moment.
It's as if once the bird has broken the image within that unforgettable photograph, that the door to the whole outside world is open. As the day begins to pollute your senses, the smell of freshly brewed coffee fills your nostrils replacing the fuchsia's and lavenders with earthly and deep dark scents. The caffeine rush is evident even in the aroma flooding out of the kitchen, filling the whole house with that 'Good Morning' smell. Praising the day you bought a percolator with a timer, you gently step up and over Sleeping Beauty and lean towards the back of the bedroom door to pull down your dressing gown to hide your birthday suit. Tying the belt around your waist you turn to have one more look at perfection still lying in the warmth it has taken you eight hours to create. She is everything you ever dreamed of, a princess in her own right. All you ever wanted.
The dogs stir as soon as you enter the kitchen, but they aren't bitter that you've woken them from whatever mystical planet they are visiting in their dreams, they are pleased to see you. Ever loyal and forever your companion, you stroke them both on the head and say good morning followed by their own individual name.
"Good Morning Ralphy, Good Morning Rosie." These dogs have become such a big part of your family, two liver and white Springer Spaniels that you rescued when a work colleagues marriage failed. Having suffered years of being ignored and nothing more than a burden, they are now thriving and prospering in a settled environment and loving home life. You are just pleased the two of you could help them, they really are like your children. The final piece in the family jigsaw.
The morning greetings done, you head towards the back door and pull it towards you quietly, opening the exit outside and into the

morning sunshine. Liberation and release, allowing the dogs the chance to escape for the first toilet stop of the day.

Stretched out in front of you and them is field after field, a haven in the middle of nowhere. You are surrounded by green grass and a hive of activity from livestock. Sheep, cows, then sheep again, then more cows. Sometimes the fields are awash with a mixture of both. However, there is one thing that doesn't change, a constant in a world ever changing. A sight that you are so familiar seeing that you no longer even notice it. The huge frame of the big black bull is always on the horizon. Always there and always watching over his flock. You pause for a few seconds absorbing the freshness and purity that only morning can bring, the dew and cobwebs that have lain so long untouched and unseen. The smell of a sweet dampness that the dawn of a new day produces and the little whir of activity from the insect world that reminds us that we are not the only ones to love this hour, in fact they remind us that in every way of life we are not the only ones. We are such little creatures in this great big enormous world.

You turn away from the open door, leaving the dogs to sniff and urinate until their hearts are content and move back into the sterile environment of the kitchen. Coffee, of course that is what has brought you here, that is what your body now craves that it has been woken and disturbed from paradise.

You stretch up towards the cupboard above the kettle and the machine responsible for such a delightful scent, opening the door you enter a world of sugar and biscuits. Ignoring temptation, as it is far too early, you force your hand past the multi colored den of calories and pick out two mugs before placing them back on the bench.

Your mug has a picture of a famous cartoon character on it, bought for you as a present by the work colleague whose dogs you ended up adopting, originally for a secret Santa but they thought it was so funny they couldn't keep their identity 'secret!' Purchased and meant in a twist of irony you hope, you pour the steaming hot coffee into your Mr Grumpy mug.

Funny how he thought the world of you though when he needed his dogs rehomed you think to yourself, a little smile come frown spreads across your face as you gently shake your head.

No milk or sugar for you, never has been, just black. Black and strong.

Her mug is different, gentler and as equally as telling. Pale yellow in colour with the picture of a Hare sitting proud and free. She loves all creatures great and small. In fact, Hares and Hedgehogs make up a huge number of the mugs in the cupboard, easily out numbering your only other one, proudly displaying the crest of your favorite football team. Tea towels and place mats match the mugs, a country kitchen at its finest.

You pour her a cup too but know it will sit on the bedside cabinet getting cold as she sleeps that little bit longer, she will appreciate the thought though, which is enough for you. You also know that the way the brew will fill the room with a deep rich aroma as she dreams the early morning away, will help her wake in the same vain as you did. Contented.

Placing the cup beside her you quietly tip toe back out of the room and check the back door. The dogs are back in and staring at the two metal bowls on the bench, wishing them to be full of their breakfast. You oblige and closing the door behind you, you shake your head and let out a little chuckle to yourself. If only life and the demands placed on you were as easy. They provide you with such happiness and mean the world to you both, yet they ask for so little in return.

Next stop is the shower, steam and vapor fill the air, a fresh smell courtesy of Lynx invades the small room. You close your eyes and listen to the hum of the extractor fan, all your senses in overload, invigorating the label says but you are not one hundred percent sure that is how you feel. Maybe you should have stayed in bed just a little longer, smothered yourself in her, sniffing her scent and nuzzling into her neck just that little bit longer.

You turn the knob stopping the water. Rubbing your eyes with the fresh soft towel you immediately jump back to the land of the living as you envelope yourself in white cotton. Today is Sunday. No work today, but you have so much to do around here. Summer is very nearly here, just weeks away from breaking through the doom and gloom of winter. The garden needs tidied, the grass needs its first cut, also you have a shed full of bulbs and seeds that need planting.

Indeed it does, but the whole house could do with a good going over. A belated spring clean and tidy is exactly what it needs, just to freshen it up. You have acquired so much junk over the cold dark winter that you really should maybe have a clear out and a few runs to the tip today. Out with the old and all of that.

But its Sunday you say to yourself deep inside your conscience. A Sunday and you are both off work together. Why would you ever want to interrupt that? You want today to last forever.

Slipping into a pair of rugged old combat shorts you quickly spray some deodorant under your arms and as you pull an old T-Shirt featuring the cover of The Smiths album Meat Is Murder over your head you leave the bathroom and head once more to where Sleeping Beauty is in slumber. Eager to catch that moment you framed earlier just one more time.

Morning has broken for the third time after you, the dogs and finally now she is awake. Head propped up on those fresh pillows, including yours to give her neck even more support, she turns to face you as she hears you enter the room. Beauty personified.

"Morning baby" she says

You just smile and lean over to kiss her rose coloured lips. You don't need to speak.

She takes a sip of her coffee and you can see the thrill on her face as she finds it's still warm.

"Ok?" you ask

"Perfect." She replies and the smile that spreads across her beautiful face is enough to put your mind at ease.

You turn away fastening the belt on your shorts, gazing out at the view, you almost can't believe that after everything, this is home for you now. You have found your paradise, your belonging, your place in the big wide world. You have found contentment and perhaps best of all, you get to share it with her.

"What are we doing today?" She asks, taking another sip of the coffee you poured for her. The thought of spring cleaning, gardening and trips to the tip quickly evaporate from your mind without you even realizing.

"Anything you want baby, anything you want."

THE JOURNEY

CHILDHOOD

As a child you didn't really have any plans about what you wanted to be, no vision of the future or blueprint for how your one and only shot at this life would turn out. A rudderless ship on a violent sea maybe, or a blank canvas. All depended on your point of view.

You were very much a normal kid from a normal family. Mother, father, two kids, two cars and a nice detached house, everything was perfect, everything was how it should be. School reports were good, you had friends, people liked you. Life was a breeze.

Those friends were indeed good friends and in fact, whilst you weren't the school jock, you certainly weren't one of the nerds either. You held your own and pulled ahead, hid behind others but stood out when you needed it. You could say you were middle of the road really, and happy to be so.

Your parents always supported you in the ways that mean the world to a child. You got the latest toys, went to see the newest movies and you always collected the latest stickers and albums.

As you grew that little bit older it progressed to the latest football shirts, the trainers in vogue at that time and the latest football boots that looked just like the ones the professionals wore in SHOOT magazine. They never made you play any better, but you gained a little respect in the PE lessons for at least looking the part.

Outside school you played for hours doing all sorts. The old fashioned street football, with jumpers for goalposts, British Bulldog if there was enough of you out and about, but your overall favorite was the classic Hide and Seek. Running around those housing estates watching your friend hunt frantically for you was always something you relished, memories now that you cherish and adore. Fun times that just never seemed to end, you were such a happy child.

The game itself didn't deviate from the text book original, but the version you enjoyed always seemed to bring you a partner, somebody to class as a companion and undoubtedly a friend. Without any planning really, you always found a hiding place that was big enough for two, whether that 'other' was male or female it didn't really matter, you always took the lead role. So even at such a young age your potential as a leader shone through. You were a doer not a pretender and this of course led to you always finding the greatest hiding places.

Kids are kids, and of course there are always some fall outs. One child had a particular hard time because she wore glasses and had a bit of a lazy eye. It wasn't Deborah's fault obviously, it was just the way she was born. Nature had dealt her a really difficult hand with her eye, but there were other medical conditions too. Things more sinister and disabling, but you never really asked or got to the bottom them. Why did it matter? You were just children.

Children can be cruel though, and after one particular nasty incident that reduced Deborah to tears, your parents received a visit from Deborah's mother in hysterics.

You hadn't really been part of inflicting the humiliation, but you were there. That was enough; guilty by association you would find out it was called later in life. Still, as you sat on the stairs and listened to both sets of parents discuss the day's events, after being sent to your room, you realised how awful you and your friends had been. Although you took no part in the mocking you felt guilty. You should have stopped it, you could have stopped it, made the humiliation go away. It would have been so easy, but you didn't. You stood back and let it go on, something hidden away in the furthest part of your mind that you would regret for the rest of your days.

The effect your group's selfish fun making had had on Deborah had led to some real issues in her life, and her mother was extremely worried.

You tried to make sure that nobody picked on Deborah again after that, you always tried to stick up for her. You made sure that she was included in all you and your gang did, even the boy's stuff. So much so that she came to every birthday party you ever had up until you were about sixteen. Always being the first invite given out, always the first to be accepted and returned.

You never spoke to her about the night her mother was in tears in your sitting room, you simply tried to make amends. However, despite appreciating your kindness she never really trusted you or anyone in her life really, she was always looking for the bitter twist or the sting in the tail. Years later you heard she had committed suicide whilst struggling to fit into a new job after a bout of depression. She was only twenty three. That guilt resurfaced the day you heard that news and never ever left. Although it clearly wasn't your fault, you still felt guilty. You could have stopped it. You should have stopped it.

Others in your group went on to prosper and do well for themselves. It's strange how you can see the adult developing from the child as if the path was laid out for them right from those early days. For example, Anthony was always going to be a lawyer from the way he controlled and governed all the games. He ran the street club amongst you, he was the law.

Molly on the other hand always had a doll with her, always taking care of something, she grew up to love kids and the last you heard she was a nursery school teacher with three children of her own. They were just kids when you knew them, but they had a plan and clearly their futures had been mapped out. Despite being such good friends at such a young and impressionable age, they were so different from you.

As you grew slightly older the games changed, the girls became less interested in football and the rough and tumble games. Hide and Seek took on a whole new level of curiosity, sometimes it even turned into curious little sexual stand off's where holding hands or a quick cuddle would sometimes come into play as the others looked for you. Your first experience of sexual excitement but you hardly even noticed. Back then the buzz was all about not being found. Ironic now that you are screaming out for somebody to find you and save you.

You had your first kiss with a girl called Marie whilst hiding behind some garages one day. Your first 'peck on the lips' is probably a better description compared to what was to come, but that early summer evening was one you would never really forget. The fact that someone could find you that attractive, even though they didn't even know what attraction was at that age. You had been wanted, and for the first time in your life there was intimate contact, a need and a value to your existence. Such a simple thing, but the difference it made was great and you liked how it made you feel. Your secret place was one that you never shared with anybody else. The little lane behind the last row of houses on your estate. All that separated the houses, lane and the field the big black Bull lived in, was the tiny little brook full of sticklebacks that hurried along on a totally different timescale to everything else.

You tried to hide with Marie the next night and every night after that in fact, but she never allowed you that privilege ever again. She never entered the lane that served as the Bull's horizon, she never let you get that close again. That perk became Anthony's, he took control again and from about the age of twelve until they were about eighteen and went to college they were inseparable.

Further education in different parts of the country provided the divide and downfall, but despite talks of a planned engagement during the summer before they went away in the first week of September, the relationship was over before October was out. Young love blown away by the temptation of others, the devil's work you used to say.

You have no idea what Marie is doing now. You'd like to think she has a family and a man who adore her. Madly in love with each other, he cherishes every kiss as much as you did all those years ago. However, deep down you know that devotion such as that does not exist, life is one man for his/herself. As a child you would never have accepted that.

Your life was turned upside down shortly after your eighth birthday when your parents separated, the resulting proceedings began in a bitter and twisted divorce. The loss of the stability of your perfect family unity came as a huge shock to such a young and innocent boy and the constant fighting and living within the battle was difficult to accept or understand. Yes, there had been arguments, but you always just presumed they made up afterwards when you went to bed. Wasn't that what grownups did? They were adults who loved each other and knew how to make everything better. They knew how to fix things and how to overcome problems, so they could pull the family back together. That's what mams and dads did. Your entire future depended on then.

Clearly this wasn't the case with your parents and when you came home to find your mother in tears and staring at a letter written in your father's handwriting you knew family life was over, your innocence taken away and that your life would never be the same again.

Your sister seemed too understand things more a little quicker than you, yet whilst at first, she began to try and explain stuff to you, she quickly became more distant as puberty and then boyfriends entered her life and filled the space in her life where her baby brother had once ruled. Just a case of growing up, it happens to everyone, but in reality, she soon left you too. You were alone, even as a child from an early age.

You too though were building relationships and when a new boy joined your class you were first to offer the olive branch of friendship. Maybe it was what had happened that day with Deborah, but when the lanky figure of Pete walked into the classroom for the first time you were drawn into making him feel extremely welcome and part of the gang. First days at a new school are notorious for being tough, but you made sure that wasn't the case for Pete and he always appreciated that.

High school provided a huge change for you all, and whilst some of you faded into the masses of other kids who had arrived from other schools, others stayed close.

You too branched out a little, evolved and made new friends who introduced you to new hobbies. Music became a big thing and one Christmas receiving a tape recorder that not only could record music direct from the radio but could also copy music from your friend's cassettes in what was known as 'high speed dubbing' meant you really did feel as if you had an unlimited library of thousands of artists. The world was suddenly accessible musically. As you broadened your horizons your views and opinions also grew. Every new song or artist you discovered made you somebody else, influenced you and changed you forever. They taught you the way of the world and made you the person you eventually became. Your musical tastes grew and matured almost as quickly as you did and from those small acorns running wild around the streets the world had whole new forests to deal with.

EDUCATION

High school was maybe the best time of your life, so many changes and discoveries as you developed both physically and emotionally. The child became a teenager, the teenager set off on his journey to become a man. It was during those five years, including your sixth form years, that the person you are today was eventually formed after surviving GCSE's, A levels, puberty and acne. You matured, with the patchwork of feelings and beliefs knitting together to provide the twisted web that still binds you today, weaving the infrastructure of you, for better or for worse.
Maybe it was even during this process that the majority of the damage internally was done, the beginning of the end, but you didn't really care then. You just lived for the moment.
The new friends you made at high school were ones that you would keep with you for the rest of your days before the fall, or most of those days when you were remotely happy anyway. They slipped away like everyone else in the end, but throughout the adolescent years and the years of becoming a man, they were there.
Anthony, Marie, Pete, they all moved onto other things. Some would say bigger and better things, but you were also changing, growing up.
One of your new friends was James, a really intelligent young man who always seemed to let himself down by trying to be the class clown. Still he made you laugh and as the years went by you often remember laughing with James in the same way you remember those Christmas's from before your parents split up. Amazing times full of cheer that seemed perfect in every way, but now they seemed to have been so long ago, that maybe you just dreamt them?
One of the greatest moments you shared was during a math's class with Mrs Stokes. You hated math's, a boring and pointless lesson that you were sure would play no further part in your existence after you left school and it especially made matters worse the fact that you didn't see eye to eye with the teacher. It seemed like none of the class really respected her and there was often a lot of talking and not a lot of listening during her lessons. Some would view this as weak teaching, but to be honest it was more about the pupils than her, to be honest she never stood a

chance. Her anger and frustration often boiled over and some poor soul often ended up paying the price for the whole class's lack of respect, usually James, by spending the rest of the lesson in the corridor where undoubtedly another teacher would see them and take them to task and therefore completely undermining her authority even further.

On this particular Wednesday afternoon James and you had been separated. He was sitting two tables in front of you and to your right. In front of him was a girl called Angela. She was the nearest you had to a class swat, and despite all of his carrying on, James was always a little jealous of this and got especially annoyed when she would volunteer to get up out of her seat to write the correct answer on the blackboard at the front of the class, much to Mrs Stokes's pleasure and the disapproval of the rest of the classmates. Both expected and loathed, Angela's actions were often the subject of the pre class chatter, increasing James's frustrations even more, after all, he was the only person to be centre of attention.

Angela's uniform was always immaculate, straight out of the catalogue. Her blouse was always diamond white, with her skirt looking as if it had been pressed to perfection before she put it on that morning. Creases never appeared in either, no matter how late in the day she grabbed the attention of the teacher. On top of her perfect attire, Angela always wore a long grey knitted cardigan. One that went down to somewhere between waist and her skinny knees. Around her waist was a long woolen belt that matched the cardigan, it always hung on each side like two limp arms trying to touch the floor, swaying every time she thrust her hand in the air exuberantly to get Mrs Stokes attention.

That afternoon the belt must have attracted James's attention more than ever and whilst the teacher was writing a huge algebra problem on the blackboard, he very gently leaned forward, backside leaving the plastic seat it called home, cleverly using his ruler he managed to hook the left side of the belt that was dangling free in such a way it was simply too much to resist. Stretching, he was able to reach over a little more and tie it around the arm of Angela's seat. Next, he repeated the act with the other end of the belt, tying it to the other arm of the chair. You noticed him tying the second one and instantly your eyes checked the other arm and you weren't disappointed. You couldn't help yourself and you let out a splutter of laughter which caused Mrs Stokes to turn around and give you a freezing stare requesting silence before she turned back to face the maze of letters and numbers. Once again, she had missed a trick and a real opportunity to show you just who was boss in that classroom.

James turned and gave you an equally chilling look as if to warn you to be quiet, this was to be his greatest moment, before that huge Cheshire cat grin spread back across his handsome face and he turned to finish the task in hand. Sitting back in his chair and obviously very satisfied with himself he turned to you and winked, clearly proud as punch with his achievement, before he turned back to face the blackboard. You both knew exactly what was going to happen next.

"Who would like to come up and write the answer on the board?" asked Mrs Stokes.

"Me miss!" Replied Angela immediately, her hand in the air so fast that your eyes didn't even have time to focus on her arm moving, just a grey blur as fast as an arrow.

Both you and James sat upright in your chairs in anticipation and in unison, waiting for it to happen. Once Mrs Stokes had nodded her permission to Angela to come forward, she bolted up except of course she couldn't stand. The home made restraints James had manufactured had worked and Angela, not knowing why she couldn't move, was like a video of a jack in the box played at twice the normal speed. Up down, up down, up down.

The whole class erupted in laughter, hysterical laughter with James making the most noise by banging his hands off his desk as tears poured down his cheeks.

Angela's face was red with embarrassment; Mrs Stokes's was red with fury. The laughter just seemed to go on and on until the teacher from the next class came in to see what was going on.

Frowning and furious, Mr Cassidy managed to hold in his laugh as he ordered James to the headmaster's office. Angela was still sitting tied to her chair as he past and left the classroom. A plan that had worked to perfection and despite knowing what he'd done was wrong; your admiration for James grew that day. Not only had he manifested the plan, he'd had the audacity to execute it and execute it very well. He too was a doer.

Another of your new friends was a girl called Trudy, a classmate in your English class that grabbed your attention the first day you saw her. There was definitely no sexual attraction there, just a curiosity as to what this girl, who always seemed to be wearing black, was all about. Trudy was the first person you ever spoke to that wore Dr Marten boots, a black leather biker jacket and often turned up to school with a collection of multi coloured streaks in her hair. She got away with most of the alternative clothes and make up most of the time, but the rainbow hairstyle usually got her sent home. She would come in the next day with her hair bleached blonde or dyed black, then the very next day she'd have another strip of vibrant colour running through it, resulting in her being sent home again. Just one big circle that the teachers never really understood or had the common sense to stop. Trudy did though, she understood the game completely. Orchestrating every move, she won every time.

This process ran for the whole of the first year in high school until one day it stopped. Trudy had decided enough was enough, but instead of conforming to the establishment and going for a nice mousey brown traditional haircut, she simply shaved her hair off, Sinead O'Connor style. None of the teachers said a word to her on that one. How could they? What could they do? Trudy had simply upped the stakes beyond anything that the teachers were prepared to match, therefore in doing so, she had finally won the game.

In class she was very much the perfect pupil. She loved literature, excelled in creative writing and had this incredible skill of being able to turn her own written work into something that really mattered. It was as if the stories she wrote depict lyrics from some obscure record or maybe even the script to a low budget independent film. Either way she had a style you liked both in her work and appearance. She was the first person to leave you intrigued, to really interest you. Somebody so cool she was right up there in that rebellious cult with Marilyn Monroe and James Dean. In that English class Trudy was the first person who really made you stop and think, the first person whoever intrigued you as to why they were so different.

One lesson on a dreary Tuesday afternoon, you were put in her group to discuss something from the book 'The Colour Purple' a book you really found difficult to connect with.

During the group discussion Trudy too seemed to drift off and you noticed she was doodling something onto the inside of the back cover of her writing book.

"Fifteen minutes with you. Well, I wouldn't say no Oh, people said that you were virtually dead, and they were so wrong."

Those words drew you in the moment you read them.

"What does that mean?" you asked trying to sound at least a little bit cool.

"Lyrics." Came a short response. You paused, your brain quickly trying to process every line of the Colour Purple in case you'd missed something, in preparation for if the teacher asked for your views, even though the only words in the whole that mattered at that moment in time were the ones written in Trudy's notebook.

"Did you write them?"

Trudy let out a laugh and quickly stifled it by putting her hand over her mouth, making you feel stupid.

"No!" she replied then a little quieter.

"Although I wish I had because they're amazing, aren't they?" she replied, you were not sure whether she was talking to you or simply asking herself.

"No, it's from a song by The Smiths. You heard of them?"

Of course, you hadn't! At that point in your life, your main focus in music had been recording the top 40 from the radio on a Sunday evening. You knew every chart topper from the last three years, but in all that time you had never heard of The Smiths or listened to words as powerful as those Trudy had just written. You so wanted to say that you had, so much so that you tried to force your head to nod, but your mouth had a different plan and instead the truth was heard.

"No." You hung your head in shame. Honesty was definitely the best policy though and for the rest of that term you spent hours at Trudy's house listening to The Smiths, The Cure, Wedding Present, The Mission, The Cult, the list of new bands, artists and genres was endless. She introduced you to a world of music that you had no idea existed, in doing so she changed you forever.

Hours of discovering new sounds, new words, new ways of writing and of seeing the world. Most of the time you'd quickly record a copy onto a cassette of all the stuff you liked but maybe hadn't heard before. By the time you called in after school the next day you knew every song word for word.
It was about this time that you started writing, trying to eclipse the heroes that you listened to religiously on those C60's and C90's. Using the pen to release your own anguish and feelings, using the pen to try and understand your own emotions.

The Common Room Ghost.

Wishing is an easy thing,
So many hopes and dreams,
Everybody does it,
All but me it seems.

Sitting in the common room,
Teenage, 'crazy' years,
Wishes wisp around their heads,
As I break down in tears.

Spending hours by my bedside,
Not planning future missions,
Reflecting on nostalgia,
Reliving ancient visions.

So this is me, the single figure you see,
Lonely, plain and dull.
Not the muscle He-man, nor the raging bull.
And this is me, the ghostly figure you see,
Gliding, pale and mysterious,
But on the outside boring and so tedious.

"The apparition of a dead person.
A specter; A disembodied spirit,
Semblance or shadow."

Living is a simple thing,

Dreaming, having fun.
But when you're 'imaginary'
In the living sense you're gone.

Sitting in the common room,
Teenage, 'crazy' years,
Wishes wisp around their heads,
As I break down in tears.

Spending hours by my bedside,
Not planning future missions,
Reflecting on nostalgia,
Reliving ancient visions.

So this is me, the single figure you see,
Lonely, plain and dull.
Not the muscle He-man, nor the raging bull.
And this is me, the ghostly figure you see,
Gliding, pale and mysterious,
But on the outside boring and so tedious.

When the soul has passed away,
On the only justice day,
When the soul has passed away,
On the only judgment day,
Then may I rest in peace.

The first meeting stayed true and even when you got to know her better there was still never any sexual tension between you and Trudy, you just became good friends. In later years you wouldn't have thought that could be possible, but your relationship really was just some kind of divine coming together, two soul mates that really had no idea how much each other needed the other. Often your evening of music would be interrupted by the latest boyfriend coming to collect her to take her somewhere in his car to do whatever older boys do with younger impressionable girls. You always disliked whoever turned up, not because you were jealous knowing they'd be making out, but because they interrupted your time with her and ultimately your musical learning! Eventually of course nature won the contest and the older boys provided more of an attraction to Trudy than you did, leading to your music sessions being stopped, way too soon in your eyes. So, with a Walkman packed with songs that would mean something to you for the rest of your life, you ventured out into the great big world that she had introduced you too and started to discover your own new bands. Whilst you fell in love album by album, artist by artist, none of them were anywhere near as special as the ones she had introduced you too.

About twenty years later you bumped into Trudy in the local supermarket, down the aisle where they keep all the cleaning potions and lotions, she had mousey brown hair and was accompanied by two small children.

After an initial awkward moment of staring and recognising someone but unsure from where, followed by more staring, you broke the silence.

"Trudy? Trudy is that you?"

Turns out that the class rebel had sold out and after her parents eventually kicked her out of the house after a succession of run ins over her choice of boyfriends, or more importantly the age of her boyfriends. She'd got a job working in the civil service on the big office park on the outskirts of town to help pay for her new flat and the living expenses of the outside world. She was still employed there to the day of your chance meeting in aisle twenty three, then she had married one of her bosses who was fifteen years her senior, before having two sons, Tom and Harry.

I think the boy's names shocked you more than anything else about her story. They were far too main stream and far too suburban housing estate for her, maybe you expected the names of the lead singers of the bands she introduced you too.

Years and years later, the emergence of social media brought about the undoubtedly bad idea of school reunions. You didn't attend any of them, but curiosity would often get the better of you, resulting in you having to search through the photographs of all the familiar faces, all a little fatter, greyer and balder, to see just who had turned up. No Angela, no Trudy but James was there, smiling and centre of attention on almost every photo. Turned out he'd done extremely well for himself in the world of corporate sales, with several homes in this country and abroad. He had never married but arrived with a beautiful woman on his arm that looked half his age, chauffeured in a brand new convertible Porsche. Mrs Stokes would have been very proud of him you thought as you sat sipping a large glass of Cabernet Sauvignon whilst staring at your tablet. You took another sip and wondered if anyone else had expected to see you there or had even been looking through the same photos as you had, just to see if they could see your face. Then reality dawned, you doubted very much whether anybody even remembered your name, never mind want to see your face.

Those years at high school really did fly over and transform you. You entered a child and after passing all your GCSE's you exited into six form developing into a man, like I've already said. Girls and cars were still to come of course, but you often look back on those friends and days and wonder if you knew what you know now back then you would have changed the way you've lived your life. Maybe if you'd been the joker like James and not stuck in at your lessons, you would have made your millions? Who knows? But then I guess you would have missed out on a musical education, a lesson in life and missed all the fun on your own journey.

Maybe the grass isn't always greener?

BOGEY MAN

There was a road next to where you grow up called Dale Road. Just an ordinary road, with ordinary families and full of ordinary semi detached houses with bay windows both upstairs and down. As a kid you used to love to walk along there, drawn to that particular street because each of the house's woodwork were painted a different colour, Rainbow Road you used to call it. The window frames and the old fashioned front doors would always be bright, the various hues would always contrast with a black border, almost Georgian in design.

There was something really special about that street when you were a child, the yellows, the blues, the greens, all the colours of the rainbow. Each one attracted your gaze, the choice of colour could maybe even tell you something special about the family that lived inside, the people who were lucky enough to live inside, what were they like? What did they do?

Everyday you'd walk home from school and although you could always cut along Front Street and then up Grainger Road and maybe save about 2 minutes from your walk home, you always chose not to. You always took the longer path and made that slight detour down Dale Road.

The gardens changed with the seasons, browns, oranges and reds then through to green, yellows and blues, before returning through the amber spectrum and finishing the year brown again. The gardens were always immaculate, but in the summer, they were simply something else.

Walking home you would often stop and sniff the air as you passed certain houses, inhaling the rich and fruity aroma of the sweet peas, the regal serenity of the lilies and the sheer beauty of the fuchsia bushes. If you had closed your eyes you could have been anywhere in the world, some far off exotic jungle surrounded by a posy of scents and the buzzing of insects subtly getting on with their day.

You would pass at least twice every day, morning and late afternoon, on your way to and from school, where often you would see the elderly residents meticulously taking care of their gardens and cutting back the shrubs and bushes, edging the flower beds, or sometimes if you'd been playing football down at Crawford Park in the evening, you would see the gentleman mow their lawns whilst the ladies cooked the evening meals, the smell of roast dinners and gravy floating down the street from house to house like that old Bisto advert on television. A hive of activity with both husband and wife getting everything in order so they could sit down together, ready for Coronation Street with a nice cup of tea in hand.

It was a quaint little life in a quaint little street, full of people who had lived there most of their lives in houses that had been in their families for years. You were still too young for life changing decisions or mapping out your future, but you often imagined yourself living there when you were really old, with a beautiful silver haired woman who would help you look after your rose garden before you'd relax together in the evening with a nice glass of red wine.

A wonderful street that was so full of charm and character, that was apart from one house near the bottom, house number 48. That particular house was the one with the big corner garden, stretching out as Dale Road swept around to the right and became Windsor Gardens. The gardens of that house were never kept nice, there was never a smell of jasmine or thyme floating up from the desperately over grown front garden. Just emptiness brought on by neglect and a sense of loss and wilderness.

Being on the corner, the plot consisted of a little more land than the other houses in the street, which made the view even worse, if you drove into Dale Road from that end it really did display as an eyesore and a blemish on an otherwise serene landscape.

The grass stretched high above the low garden wall that protected the house's boundaries, thistles and nettles blotting the horizon in a beautiful but volatile fashion. You would have to be a very brave child to hop that wall and wade through the garden of toxins to get your football if someone's missed placed pass or wayward shot had breached security. The purple and deep blues of the thistle heads a sheer and beautiful distraction to the venomous spikes and leaves that lived underneath.

The garden had been attended in some way though and around the edges of what was once lawn there was a second little barrier thou shall not cross. Only this defence system was so unique and relentless, it was nothing short of bizarre.

Behind the defensive line of bricks and thistles, there was a hub of little mini circles made up of smaller mini circles which in turn decorated and made shape of an otherwise forgotten wasteland.

The first time you were brave enough to peer over the wall at the sun glistening off the silver discs, you saw that they all contained symbols. Every single piece of the very messy jigsaw had a sign on it, an emblem, more importantly an emblem which made each one different from the next despite initially all looking like replicas of each other. You recognized the graphic on one, then on another, then another.

BMW, Audi, Ford and Vauxhall. Just a few of the badges you recognised from what your brain now realised were wheel trims, like the ones that were fitted to your father's car, although you couldn't see any Nissan ones that were an exact match for your family's mode of transport, realisation meant that suddenly something that had seemed a daunting wall of defence had a look of familiarity about it. The fascination and intrigue grew as the fear subsided.

The wheel trims became an obsession, everyday on your way home from school you would stop and look at the hundreds that were strategically placed around the garden and every day you seemed to discover a new one or discovered a new emblem.

In turn you started to look at the wheels of parked cars as you walked down other streets, trying to put the manufacturer's names to the signs and learn new ones. Your knowledge of car manufacturers grew immensely, but, never did you ever find one that matched the ones on your car at home.

As you hurried through the terms of school and growing up you began visiting the garden of 48 Dale Road even more, making mental pictures of the formations and placements these wheel trims had been arranged, trying to work out the puzzle. Not even knowing that you were doing it most days, you just subconsciously used what was there in front of you for so many of your day to day school tasks.

During one art project at school you sketched as many of the car manufacturers logo's as you could see, placing each and every one into a blurred background that symbolised that they had no real need or purpose to be there. They just were, just like 48 Dale Road.

During Geography one time, you were sent out to do a traffic count, a kind of survey to register the most popular car within your little town. Not the most stimulating project, but in accepting it was how they were expected to spend a Tuesday afternoon, all the other kids in your class rushed to nearby junctions, roundabouts and traffic lights. You however, had different plans, making sure nobody saw where you were heading, you put your head down as you left through the school gates and ran all the way to Dale Road. Standing on the safe side of the wall you counted every wheel trim in number 48's garden. Ford was undoubtedly the most popular with Audi and then Vauxhall next. Insignificant results, but to you they clearly meant something. You sat break after break, night after night trying to work out some kind of pattern. There must be a reason why they were displayed in that way? Why there were certain manufacturers more popular than others? You never worked it out. No matter how hard you tried. Likewise, the teacher never questioned your results and, why would he? You'd filled the form in like all the other kids.

That little unkept blot on an otherwise idyllic piece of paradise became your special place, a place you could go to think, a place that you could go to draw, a place you could go to be on your own, but of course you were never completely on your own. You just thought you were.

You began to go more and more and, instead of just passing and going around the corner on your way home you began to pay more attention to the whole plot rather than just the garden and the alien like decor it had built up over the years, each piece of somebody's treasure reflecting the sun and spraying its rainbow rays off in all directions, cascading beautiful prisms of magical colour that simply fascinated you and drew you in deeper.

You began to notice more details the more you went. The different forms of vegetation that was hidden under the waist length grass, the rusty swirls of the creaky gate and features of the house itself, such as the very bricks that created it. Worn, old and red some had cement missing from in between them. Some you could see had the names of the manufacturers on at some point, both now corroded away over the years from the aggressive sea atmosphere and years of a lack of maintenance.

You noticed the old trellis next to the front door that only homed the skeletal remains of a long dead clematis. The stems of the once vibrant plant, just grey and dry, dead from the roots up over. Nobody had taken the time to water it and nobody had bothered to put it out of its misery. Instead it was left to hang there, woven into the wooden trellis as if it was holding the whole house up. Who knows, maybe it was.

The most obvious contrast between number 48 and the other houses in the row though was the lure that had attracted you to the street in the first place. The rainbow paint jobs of windows and doors that had attracted your attention almost from the minute you first set your eyes on them. The sheer beauty and brightness, the candy cane effect, those doors and window frames had drawn you right in from day one, almost like the long line of beach huts that decorated the coast line not too far away. However, it was the macabre black frames and door of number 48 that had captured your imagination from that point on. No bright colour to compliment the black piping, all of the house's paintwork was a dull and dirty looking black. Not a shiny black like the colour of Mr Townsend's new Ford Fiesta two doors down, the paintwork was flat and weathered. Simply dead black.

Flaking at the edges, you could see that the paintwork had always been black, layer after layer of darkness, as the woodwork shed its skin like a sunburned holiday maker.

Black and dull, dirty and flat. That was the words you used to describe the house when writing about it in an English assignment one day. You entitled the piece 'Death and Decay' though at that point you had no idea why it seemed such a good fit.

You never saw anyone come or go from number 48, you weren't even sure that anyone even lived there, which in turn just added to the mystery, intrigue and obsession.

One day curiosity got the better of you, and you decided to violate the clear boundaries and cross through the poison garden for a closer look. Adrenalin pumping you waded through the nettles and thistles, the weeds and thorns, your school bag becoming a shield as you double it up and used it like a snow plough to part them, but it was a losing battle as more and more

sprung up taking the place of the previous one, like a den of Cobras on the attack.
You could feel the stings through your school trousers and, at one stage you are sure heard a little rip in the rear of your jacket as you passed a little jungle of Hawthorn bushes. You couldn't see any damage when you pulled the garment around to look, but deep down you knew somewhere the jacket had ripped, leaving a permanent scar and a long lasting reminder of your time here. Now there was a trace, even if only you knew it, which was the last thing you wanted.
Having trudged across a plain of knots and spikes that seemed to go on forever, you finally hit a more permanent ground, pushing back a twisted pile of leaves you saw you had reached a concrete path that wound around the downstairs bay window.
Your heart was racing, as beads of perspiration began to form on your forehead and under your pre-puberty arms. What were you doing there? Why didn't you just stay on the safe side of the wall? Why didn't you look into the hundreds of wheel trims and see your reflection and realise this was no place for you? Why, oh why. Instead you were just inches from the most frightening house you had ever seen. Just inches, but that isn't even the crux of it. You were standing right outside the main eye of the house, the all seeing eye, the downstairs bay window.
For the 30 seconds when you were standing there, your eyes had been tightly jammed closed. You could feel the pulse in your temple pounding with both fear and excitement. You had come so far, risked everything. Surely you needed to look inside? But then what if you opened your eyes and there was someone else there, inside staring out at you? Just waiting for you to open your eyes so they could pounce. After all, you were on their property, this was their world.
Seconds passed again, you knew you had to do something. You couldn't just stand there frozen forever.
Counting to three you opened your eyes, slowly turning towards the gaping mouth of the window expecting it to swallow you up, to take you alive.
The nerves and excitement though had been a waste of energy and you let out a huge sigh of relief and tension when your eyes saw nothing but black and darkness. Black because the curtains

were drawn. You couldn't see inside and more importantly inside couldn't see you. You let out a little gasp, breath taken from you in relief and without asking permission your eyes begin to survey the inside of the bay. Curious and busy they flitted from side to side of the expanse that stood in front of you. Desperate to spot something but they were also terrified something may spot you.

Dead flies littered the window sill like some medieval battle ground, slain and forgotten, you wondered if the side they gave their life for was victorious or defeated, but deep down you knew the answer to that. Hundreds of them gone, leaving nothing but a sun baked, crisp shell of a body to let people know that something alive was once where there was now death. As if to give out a warning.

Panning the horizon in front of you, more cautiously and a little more thoroughly, your eyes scoured the yellow sun stained gloss paint that seemed to stretch on for as far as you could see. Then it clicked, you noticed that the flies weren't the only things that had taken up occupancy of the windowsill. Feeling both slightly more relaxed and curious, your eyes began to cast further afield from straight ahead, there had to be something else there, something that symbolised life. It was on that further exploration that you realised rather spookily there was another creature decorating the polluted gloss paintwork. Every 10 centimeters or so, each gap looking identical to the naked eye, was a series of figurines. Everyone the same, everyone black. Dotted right along the entire duration of the gloss work was a 'herd' of alabaster bulls.

Stretching the entirety, they were all the same, except the one right in the middle, the one that was holding the whole display together. That model was bigger and more prominent, the ring leader casting a watching eye over all the others, big and dominant, he was watching over everything. One you noticed him you couldn't stop looking at him. His gaze was fixed on you, sucking you in towards him so that nothing else mattered. Black like all the others, it was the creature's bright red eyes that seemed to be staring right at you that freaked you out the most. Hypnotic and translucent they stayed in your subconscious mind forever, always the lure into darkness and the deep.

Head spinning you turned and ran, leaping through and over the prickly plants with some strange gait that certainly wouldn't have won you any Olympic prizes. You knocked over several wheel trims on your way out of the garden as you performed the long jump to get over the small garden wall, but you just kept on running. There was no time to look back, no time to erase the trail you had left through the wheel trims, you had been there long enough and seen enough, there was no way you were going to stop and look back. If you had you may have seen the long crooked finger and dark hazel eye peering around the pulled back, black curtain in the upstairs bedroom. Watching emotionless and in silence, observing you destroy everything that it had created.

"Why do you hang around that creepy old house on Dale Road so much?" James asked you out of the blue one day as you made the daily trip along Front Street to Melvin's, the local newsagents that also happened to keep a little hot box stuffed with sausage rolls, pasties and the like, all the things that kids loved. Thus, the shop was a firm favorite of all the pupils at school, with little groups of the various years stood outside on dinnertimes. The older kids sometimes used to sneak a sly cigarette outside, as they tried to illustrate to the younger ones just how grown up and cool they were.

Such a pointless exercise to you though, as you were never interested in the older kids or smoking, the thing that attracted you to Melvin's most was the old rotating stand in the far corner of the shop, the one that held the old 7" records from juke boxes. The centre of the disc was missing, from their working days, hence they were sold off cheap. You viewed these discarded discs as real pearls, as your record collection grew and grew, often they had a few scratches thrown in for the authentic crackling juke box effect.

"It's really weird you know?" James continued, staring straight at you in a way that made you feel a little uncomfortable.

"What is?" You asked back, as you tried to divert pressure away from you.

"That house, you hanging around there, the old guy that lives there...."

"Someone lives there?" You asked, a spark illuminated inside your head and suddenly interested, you were now the one that was doing the staring.

"In number 48? Someone lives at number 48?" Your voice increased in pitch with excitement.

James stopped in his tracks and took a step back.

"You are kidding right? You do know the story about that place don't you?" James's voice put an emphasis on the word do, making those two letters sound so massive, so daunting.

"No... no I don't, I just thought it was an old empty house. I didn't think someone actually lived there." You stuttered, thinking about the other day when you gave into temptation and entered the Garden of Eden. Panic streaked through your veins, what if you were seen?

James rolled his eyes back into his head, just as you reached the door of Melvin's.

"Hang on, let me get a sausage roll and I'll tell you all about it." He said slapping you on the back like an old sailor about to tell you the wonders of the seven seas. Numb with fear and curiosity, you didn't enter the shop that day, you'd lost your appetite and even the vinyl treasures in the corner didn't appeal.

What if someone or something had seen you? You slumped against the shop window, back pressed up against the glass, and waited.

Five minutes passed, then James was out of the shop and whilst peeling down the paper bag, so he could eat his giant sausage roll like you would a banana, he silently ushered you to car park at the back of the shops and plonked his frame on top of one of the grey concrete bollards. You followed suit, although with not having anything in your hands you found it quite awkward to decide where to put them. Eventually you decide just to sit on them, at least then they couldn't get in the way.

"Well" he said, ramming more processed meat into his mouth "the guy that lives there used to be a doctor, right? So, he comes home from a long shift one evening, he'd been at work for like 15 hours at least. I think there'd been a huge car crash or something." Casting a thoughtful gaze into the distance for a second as if to confirm his own theory and to fully picture the carnage. He was certainly going to enjoy telling you this story. More sausage roll to the mouth, then whilst still chewing it James gave a little nod and then continued with his story.

"Yeah there was this massive accident right, people dying all over the place, and our doc had to work for hours. Anyway, he finally did get finished and rushed home to see his wife and kids."

Enthralled you wanted to be nearer, closer to the horror. So, without noticing you had done it, you left the safety of the bollard a few metres away and sat yourself down on the concrete stool right next to James. You were glued to his every word, wanting to know more. The position of your hands was no longer a worry. You now had greater concerns.

"No one knows what happened next really, but the next day when the postman knocked to deliver a parcel he noticed blood splashed all over the downstairs window."

"The bay one?" you asked thinking how close you had gotten to it, picturing all the little model bulls that ran along the grubby windowsill. The only death you'd witnessed was a mass fly homicide!

"Yeah, yeah" James nodded but his tone was very dismissive. "Like blood up the curtains, the walls, everywhere." Reveling in the narration of his own horror story.

You stared at James, completely transfixed on his every word. Your attention was so intense, you were watching his lips move and anticipating the words that were about to come out. You saw the movement before you heard the sounds. If you had concentrated in class like that you'd be top of the set no problem.

"So, the postie calls the police who arrive in just a couple of minutes, blue lights flashing and sirens blaring, just like tv." James waved his arms around to signal the chaos before he continued.

"There's no reply at the door so they have to kick it down." James paused for the final bite of his sausage roll. It seemed to take him ages to chew, you urged him to hurry it, to get back to his story but it was as if he knew how desperate you were and therefore stretched his snack break out as long as he could, enjoying every moment of having you hanging there. Eventually he swallowed the last piece and continued.

"When the police got in they saw the guys wife lying in a pool of blood in the passage, a hand shaped trail of blood stopped just millimeters from the phone, which has been knocked off the hook. In the sitting room is the oldest child, a boy I think it was, had his head completely caved in, with a broken dining chair strewn on the carpet next to his lifeless body. The carpet was covered in crimson splash marks and around the remains of the kid's head was a huge bloody circle. Like a halo man." At this point James hung his head for effect, as he softly shook it from side to side.

You were in complete shock, you didn't expect any of that, but hearing the details and picturing it in the room you were looking into just as recent as the other day made you feel physically sick.

"Go on" you said in a voice so soft and broken you didn't even know if the sound that came out of your mouth was audible. Regardless of whether it was or wasn't, James somehow understood and continues on, his eyes were rigid with concentration, intensely they stared straight into yours.

"So, then the coppers moved upstairs and just on the landing at the top of the stairs was the little girl. She too was lying face down, her school dress soaked beyond recognition with the blood that seconds earlier had ran through her veins. Tell you man, it was fucked up."

"Where was he?" you stuttered "where was the guy?"

"Ah well that was the sick part. They found him in the bathroom. In the bath actually, with the taps running and him covered in claret too. He was gibbering on, talking rubbish you know, saying something outrageous about how the Bull did it. I mean for fucks sake what a crazy fucker. The Bull did it!!" James laughed and jumped off the bollard, threw his paper wrapper into a nearby bin basketball style and turned back towards you.

"Slam dunk!" he shouted, a huge grin of satisfaction spreading across his face.

"What happened next? What happened to the guy??" you asked, your voice jumped up an octane as your heart pounded in your chest like a bass drum on a dance record. You could not leave until you had heard the full story.

"Is he still in the house?"

"What? Ah the loony you mean? Yeah, he was taken to hospital for a while, like a hospital for nutters, and eventually they sent him home."

"And what about the murders? Why wasn't he sent to jail?" your chest began to tighten as you asked, terrified of what he might say.

"No proof. Turns out there was a load of cash kept under the bed in a suitcase along with some jewelry. Police put it down to robbers and let him off. It was clearly him though, he must have just lost the plot. No one has ever seen him since. They say he only comes out during the night when he just messes around with those stupid wheel trims. Guys a lunatic I tell you. You need stop hanging about there or you'll become a lunatic too! Or even worse. If he catches you he'll smash your head in with a chair!"

James leaned over at that point and slapped you on top of your head, giving you a shock, before he was off.

"Come on let's go."

You stood there totally transfixed, with so many questions left to ask, but he had switched his attention to the group of girls in the year below you that had just exited the shop, bags full of sweets in their hands. As he flirted with them you walked back to school behind them in silence, you'd no interest in girls after what you'd heard, all you wanted to do is get through the afternoons lessons and go back to the house. You needed to see where it happened, you needed to see if you could find any droplets of blood on the glass in that bay window. You even wanted to see if you could catch just a glimpse of the doctor.

After school James asked if you wanted to hang out, but you said you needed to go home. He didn't argue but you suspected that he didn't believe you. Walking past Crawford Park some other boys in your class ask if you wanted to join them in a game of 3 a side, there was only five of them and they desperately needed another to be able to recreate their version of the previous Saturdays Match of the Day. Again, you declined, you had more important business to attend to, you had to return to 48 Dale Road.

You scurried down the streets and eventually reached the corner where you could see the house. You stood on the other side of the road for several minutes, your eyes took in every detail, searching for a dried blood spot or the broken chair. Of course, there was neither, why would there be James was probably telling a huge lie anyway. There's no way if someone had been found like that they wouldn't have been sent to jail. He certainly wouldn't have been sent home, sent back here.

That final thought seemed to fill you with a little more confidence, made you braver as you crossed the road heading to the house of horrors. You approached it directly and like a magnet it drew you towards it, reeling you in like a fish on a line.

You reached the rusty cast iron gate and instead of hurdling the wall, this time you simply pushed the gate open. There was a large squeak and a load of flaky paint descended from the hinges like snowflakes in a blizzard. In the eerie silence that you hadn't noticed previously the shrill of the gate made you jump and with a jolt you realised exactly what you were doing and where you were. That calmness and direction had gone and as you tried to place in your head the best thing to do next, your eyes focused on the bay window, the one that had apparently been splattered with blood.

Standing there staring straight back at you was the figure of a man. A thin, lean man, the afternoon sun reflecting back off the gold buttons of his cardigan. You looked at his streamline waist and worked up his body. Under his woolen cardigan there was a white shirt with little brown and blue checks on it. Sticking out of the open collar was a few silver chest hairs, above that a neck so wrinkly it resembled the neck of a turkey, but it was what was at the end of that neck that drew your eyes even deeper.

The face of an old man, brown skin and silver bristles decorate his chin. His face looked weathered, his cheeks gaunt. Staring right back at you was a man who had seen life in every aspect, lived through it all and was still standing to tell the tale. But would he ever tell his story? Would the truth ever come out?

For at least ten seconds your gazes were magnetic and fixed. Connected, you were staring in total shock at him whilst he was even more shocked to be looking at you. His eyes were hazel and incredibly soft. Certainly not the eyes of a deranged mass murderer, the wrinkles around them were deep set like canyons in the desert. Worry lines set in stone forever. This face hadn't smiled for a long time, none of them were laughter lines.

Tick, tock another couple of seconds passed, you and him frozen in time for what could be an eternity. You could have been the only person his eyes had set upon for years. Then like a mirror falling to the floor the ambiance was shattered like glass by such a simple, miniscule gesture, but to both of you it was mind blowing.

Without taking his eyes from yours, the old man raised his right hand. Taking what seemed like an age for your brain to process, he stretched his fingers and then closed them again. Then he repeated it and on the third gesture he slowly moved the hand from side to side. This old frail man who supposedly butchered his family in cold blood was waiving at you, he was trying to be your friend.

You didn't waive back, you didn't freeze, you turned and ran, terrified. Your body in self preservation mode, you didn't think about how your actions would make the man feel, his gesture rejected, instead you pushed all of your energies into leap frogging the garden wall, cola cubes flew from your pockets in all directions ricocheting off the wheel trims before they were lost forever in the deep forest of nettles and weeds.

Once over that wall you didn't turn around to look back at the scene you had fled, you didn't even think about doing so, you ran all the way home without stopping.

You never ever walked down Dale Road again.

CONFIDENCE

To you Northumberland Street was expansive, endless and massive. Yet you were so small and insignificant, in that environment you meant nothing. Thousands walked its millions of paving slabs, the majority suited and booted, almost everyone off to their place of work. Each one immaculately dressed, everyone was so busy, everyone was so important.

Then amongst the hustle and bustle there was you. You had been walking along this street at exactly the same time every morning for the last three days. Every day since you started this job, everyday since your vision had been engulfed by suits, suits and suits.

Thousands of people trekked along these paving slabs with you. As you walked head down, you couldn't stop thinking that they were all staring at you, looking at you knowing you didn't belong with them. You were out of your comfort zone, out of familiar surroundings. The simple fact was you were out of your depth, emotionally and physically.

Acne had spread across your face like flies splattered on a windscreen, your self esteem felt as if it has been hit by an articulated lorry. You were nothing more than road kill on the A1, everyone else was the juggernauts.

They were just all so smart and whilst you didn't know if the suits they were wearing were designer or Burtons, you did know that the one you were wearing, that you were bought for your cousin's wedding, was hanging off you like one of those little football strips on a coat hanger and suction pad that hang on the rear windows of people's cars. Oversized and a bad fit, just like you in the society that surrounded you.

You felt out of place and awkward, alone and worthless. Compared to these successful and happy people you were nothing. You couldn't lift your head to look at the others, you didn't want them to see you.

A man in a long coat and carrying a brief case tried to push past you, talking rapidly on his mobile phone, his ariel pulled out to the extreme to get the best signal. He gave you a look of disapproval as you stepped from one side to the other, unfortunately matching his movements. Eventually he threw out a hand and pushed you the opposite way to the direction he was stepping, shaking his head as he moved on he looked you up and

down and tutted in total disgust. He was far too important for you to have gotten in his way.
"What a pathetic specimen" you heard him say, but he didn't really. It was just right there in your head.
You didn't belong there, but you very much doubted that you belonged anywhere, not with your face looking so unclean, so far detached from pure and infected.
Women in business suits seemed to be everywhere, stilettos clip clopping along the path at a pace that sounded like the fastest army of miniature horses ever and, although you walked with your head down you still managed to catch a glance of the black seams up the stocking legs of a petite brunette who clearly had somewhere very important to be, or someone very important to be with.
You would have died if she had noticed you looking, she would have been disgusted if she thought you even found her slightly attractive, such a vile and hideous being should not be aloud to have such thoughts of sexual desire let alone lusting after her.
Trying to distract yourself, you caught a glimpse of your reflection in HMV's window as you were looking at that week's new releases. Your hair was all wrong. You'd spent an eternity that morning trying to get the right look, so long in fact that you had almost missed the metro train. You'd recently switched from using hair gel to Bryl Cream and at that moment as your pale and spotty complexion gazed back at you from behind the multiple covers of Nirvana's Nevermind album, which was making up the huge window display, you felt greasy. Greasy, spotty and putrid. Your own reflection sent waives of repulsion through your body and if you had this effect on you, how could you possibly ever expect anybody else to find you attractive.
Kurt Cobain's face had taken over the whole double window of the display. He had recently killed himself by shooting himself in the head. Why? When he was so perfect? It should have been you that died, not one of the beautiful people with the whole world as his oyster. You would have given anything to be him or anything even like him.
You walked further down Northumberland Street, passing Greggs and Collectables, stopping at WH Smith's to buy some chewing gum and a copy of that week's NME, you brushed your teeth

before you left home and ran for the metro, but your mouth was so dry with anxiety that you thought mints might just be useful. As if something so simple could make being with you bearable? You ran for the metro, fuck, what if you smelt of sweat now? Panic swept across the inset of your head which simply made you perspire even more. You had used nearly a full tin of the Lynx deodorant from the box set you got for your birthday from Aunty Julie in just the few days of that week. You wish you'd brought it with you and then you could have given your armpits a quick spray in the toilets before you started work. Such a simple thought that would have saved you so much stress and worry. Why didn't you think of that before you left!

For a moment you considered running back up the street the way you came to stop at Boots to buy some more, but a quick look at your watch told you that wasn't an option. Maybe on your dinner break you could nip out and buy some? Time and sheer existence, like everything else that day was against you.

The call centre was based in a building opposite the railway station, you were really going to have to step it up to get there and signed in by 9am.

So that morning it was your turn to hurry past people, but you weren't as pushy or forceful as everyone else was that had bustled past you earlier and, you drew the line at physically maneuvering people out of the way. Weak and non-assertive, so typical of you.

You arrived at the pedestrian crossing opposite the Odeon cinema and true to fashion the little stick man on the electronic display flicked from green to red just as you approached. You should have put money on that and then you would have been able to buy as much Lynx as you needed. You were about to chance it and run across the road when you suddenly slammed on the anchors as a big yellow and white double decker bus came hurtling around the corner missing your newly purchased Dr Marten shoes by inches.

Your Mam wouldn't let you wear your sixteen holer's for work. You had to look professional she had said, but that's all you'd worn since the days you spent in Trudy's bedroom, whether it had been your black or ox blood ones. You really didn't feel comfortable in anything else, but when you looked down towards

your feet that had so very nearly just lead you to your death, you were at least grateful that a compromise had been reached.
You felt little beads of sweat break out on your forehead, your pulse began to race as you waited impatiently for the little man to flash green. Red, red, constant red.
"Hurry up man, for fucks sake." You muttered under your breath, or at least you thought you had.
You felt a gaze burning a hole in the back of your head and as you turned to see who the fixation belonged to, you saw that behind you were two nuns on their way to the cathedral on the next block maybes, both stared straight back into your eyes and shook their heads. Feeling even more of a disgrace you quickly turned back to the crossing and fixed your eyes on the little man. Go green, go green you said over and over in your head, making sure you had not made the same mistake again and said the words out loud. Not only did you need to get to work, but now you needed to get away from two disapproving nuns. How you wished you were back doing your A Levels, how you wished you were anywhere but there at that time, anywhere, the garden of 48 Dale Road even. Anywhere but there.
Finally, the crossing beeped, the light became green and traffic on both sides of the road ground to a halt. You hardly noticed though, you heard the beep and from a standing start you were off, ready, steady, go! Off you set across the road heading towards the Central Station, leaving the disapproving nun's way back in the distance still discussing your atrocious choice of language.
The security guard on the door at work was called Brendon. He seemed a nice old guy, he'd been there for years and was planning to retire in the new year. His silver hair was always immaculately combed into a side parting, a perfect line revealing his pale scalp, he reminded you so much of your grandad in the photograph your mam had had displayed on the fire place for years.
Brendon always spoke to the staff member as they entered and left the building, he always had a smile and something to say, even if it was just commenting on the day's news. Not when you passed though, he never had anything to say when you made an appearance. You didn't even get eye contact most days. You

were convinced that whenever he saw you approach he would desperately seek out that day's crossword, the one he'd put down hours ago because he was stuck and had gone as far as he could, then he would proceed to look engrossed, rubbing his chin with one hand in a ponder or scratching his temple with the old yellow and black HB pencil he always used. He always looked busy and pleasant, contented and happy in his job. Brendon was living in a world completely alien to the one you were in.

Today was no different, why would it be? No small talk just the silence and a quick glance at the big rotary clock that was positioned behind his desk in reception. You could almost taste the disapproval that greeted your late arrival.

You got to your desk at ten seconds to nine and quickly threw yourself into your work station, heart and soul. Although in reality nothing could have been further away from the truth. You multitasked, as you logged onto your computer and unpeeled your suit jacket, you finally got on line about twenty seconds late. Your manager, Clifford, glanced up from behind his cream coloured computer monitor and shook his head. You could definitely taste his disapproval just like the cheese toastie that you had rammed down your neck for breakfast, the very same toastie that was deliberately repeating on you having taken offence to the extra little bit of exercise for the day in the sprint up the eight flights of stairs that took you to your desk.

Clifford's glance was enough to make your stomach sink once more, as the realisation that you didn't belong there struck home. You didn't belong anywhere, but then there was a beep in your headset as the first call of the day came through, the first of a long line of many.

VIRGINITY

The first time you fucked was a messy affair that was over before it really began, but you guessed that the majority of people could say the same thing.

A new girl had joined the office and, despite a series of girlfriends throughout school and sixth form, none of them had aroused passions and desires like you felt when Charlotte walked into the workplace that day.

She was simply gorgeous, slim, brunette and clearly out of your league, but that didn't stop you falling in love the minute you saw her. A love deep and true, but one that was never going to be. Her boyfriend dropped her off that first morning in his Ford Escort XR3i, red with blacked out windows, he looked as if he was at least four or five years older than you and her.

The familiarity between her and the only other girl you had ever gotten close too, even if it was just plutonic, Trudy, awoke memories you'd thought had long been left behind. Older men, cars and all that came with them, why did it always happen to you? Why did you always pick the ones you could never have?

"Probably sells drugs to afford a car like that!" Mavis the office cleaner said one morning as she tendered to the huge cheese plant that blocked the majority of the view from the huge office window. If it hadn't been there you may just have been able to see Charlotte and the 'undesirable' boyfriend in the bright red status symbol that had aroused Mavis's suspicions! Instead you let your imagination run wild and jump to all sorts of conclusions, externally you just nodded in agreement with Mavis. Every morning was the same, Charlotte made a dramatic arrival through the office door, quickly she unbuttoned her coat and threw it over the back of her swivel chair, switching her PC on at the same time.

Charlotte was nearly always late for work, in fact she was late everyday without exception, but she carried off her ritual of bad time keeping exceptionally well. Executing every stage of trying to look as if she had been in the office for ages with so much conviction that her lateness became impressive in its own right. Anyway, you would have never of dreamt of dropping her in it or telling tales. You loved looking at her face across your desk too much. She really had won your heart, but then she won hearts where ever she went.

The relationship between you and her was complicated and difficult for a young man full of testosterone to comprehend. She sat directly opposite you, so she had to talk to you, but did she even like you?

You talked about all sorts of things and you never felt under any pressure. Whether it was the latest limited edition flavour of her favorite thing, a KitKat, or how annoying she found her last call, every conversation ended in a smile and a giggle. Not just from you either. You were never really one hundred percent sure, but deep down you thought that she liked the chit chat you shared as much as you did.

Sometimes, if lady luck was shining on you, you were both on the same lunch break and instead of rushing out of the building and listening to your walkman in Georges Square, you would spend the full half hour in the canteen listening to the trail and tribulations of being such a beautiful woman with an older boyfriend. Girl talk really, but you would do anything to be near her and listen to her beautiful voice. Some of the tales made your not quite stubbly cheeks flush with warm, red embarrassment. Some of the other tales you simply didn't understand, especially the ones about her boyfriend shouting at her and not calling. Why would he do that? If she was your girl, you would treat her like a princess.

If only she was you girl.

One Monday dinnertime, just before Halloween, she confides in you a secret that normally she would have saved for her best friend, but she was on a different lunch schedule that week, so she turned to the next best thing and had confided in you.

Her and Colin had broken up. She had gone to his friend Ryan's house for a Halloween party on Saturday night, they'd been drinking and after not being able to see him around for a little while she ventured out into the garden. Crowds of people swigging lager and smoking cigarettes, laughing and joking amongst each other whilst all dressed as ghouls, ghosts or zombies. As they lurked around, wasted, Charlotte began to wonder how many of the figures she saw were real specters and how many were simply in costume.

On the park bench type seat, over near the garden shed, a couple she didn't know were snogging passionately. So passionately in

fact that he had one of her breasts slipped out of her Morticia costume for the whole world to see. She however didn't seem to notice or even mind, as her hand groped the erect penis that had certainly come to life under his brown hessian mad monk costume.
Disgusted even more and feeling lonely and vulnerable, she turned and headed back into the house. Darting straight through the kitchen, Charlotte headed directly towards the front door, but as she reached the end of the passage that lead to the porch and then her exit route, she paused.
"Fuck it I'll just go home." She muttered under her breath, rolling her beautiful hazel eyes back into her head.
"Maybe I should nip to the toilet first." She said resigning herself to the fact that despite standing there dressed as Buffy the Vampire Slayer, her boyfriend had rejected her, resulting in her night being almost over before it had even begun. Time for her to accept the rejection and go home.
Slowly and dejected she started to mount the staircase up towards the toilet, passing the family portrait photographs that lined the wall. Each one displayed the grinning faces of people she didn't know, all mocking her it seemed, all of them smiling as if they knew the truth that was about to unfurl.
Reaching the top of the staircase Charlotte was about to turn to her left and enter the first door she had come across. Not due to any sixth sense or mystical power, but her insight was purely down to the tacky WC sign that someone at some point had stuck on the door. However, using some kind of sticky pads, they really hadn't given the whole operation much thought as it was so wonky that even Charlotte in her desperate state to leave let out a little chuckle.
That expression of happiness was quickly removed from her face though, as just seconds later she heard grunting and groaning coming from the next door along the landing. Grunting and groaning she had heard so many times before.
Stepping past the bathroom door and in a mixture of shock and anger, she put all of her might into pushing what is obviously a bedroom door open. Opening the door onto a most hideous sight.
Colin fucking Ryan's sixteen year old sister. Watching him bang her hard and fast, her lasting memory was the boy band posters

on the wall as her vision descended into a blur of devastation and tears.

Running down the stair case she pushed past Ryan and one of his sister's female friends, hand in hand and obviously on their way upstairs to join Colin and the family. She didn't even notice them, turn and look at her, mouths wide open, as she rushed out of the front door. Tears' poured down her cheeks, ruining her mascara, they left a slimy black snail trail running down her face. Her young life had just been disintegrated for the first of many times. Everything she had that made her seem like an adult was gone, stolen and ripped into a million pieces. Her heart and spirit completely smashed, everything she thought she ever wanted was gone. How could she ever recover from that? The whole world would hear about what had happened, everyone would know, how could she possibly come back from being let down so badly? She would never be able to recover.

So, the next lunchtime in the call centre canteen Charlotte opened her heart and relayed this story back to you. All you wanted to do was hold her close as the tears streamed down her beautifully defined cheeks. All you wanted to do was lean over and kiss her passionately and tell her that everything would be alright and that she deserved better than him anyway and, that if she was your girlfriend you would never treat her like that. You would make her feel so special, so loved.

Being with her this close and her being so personal felt so right for you. It was right then that for the first time in your life you felt that feeling and knew it was true. You were in love. You moved forward, arms half extended as if to give her a cuddle. You didn't even know it yourself, but your lips started to pucker up ready to give her a kiss.

"Ah Charlotte" You said "You deserve....."

Then Amy from your team walked over and plonked her dinner tray down with a clatter, symbolically nudging yours back to your side of the table as she did.

"So how was the party last night?" She asked sticking a chicken tikka wrap into her big fat mouth.

Charlotte didn't reply. She had one last little look towards you and then burst into tears, before she stood up and then rushed out of the canteen.

Right there and then, at that very moment you could have easily killed Amy. Through your mind an image flashed of you picking up that dinner tray and slamming it right into her esophagus with such force that it instantly slit her throat, her tongue still flapping about trying to talk as you watched the life drain out of her. She had just blown your perfect moment, your one chance, she had just destroyed the woman you loved with one question. Physically shaking your head, both in disbelief and to get the image of Amy's massacre out of your head, you turned towards the direction Charlotte had run too, maybe you could still give her that hug, but she was gone.
So instead you turned towards Amy to tell her what she had just done but you didn't bother. She was too busy stuffing the rest of her wrap into that big mouth of hers. You pushed your tray back into hers, but she didn't notice that either, as you stood up and walked away.
Two days later it was the office Halloween party. You were a little nervous about going at first, everyone from work would be there including all the bosses, but you go along with the jamboree as it gathers pace in the week before the event. Everyone talking about nothing else and of course their costumes. You felt like a kid again back at school for the build up to Christmas. All that was missing was the opportunity to take in your favorite toy. Some clever sod in the HR department had had the idea of using the regional event as a good excuse to raise money for charity, some hospice somewhere that you had never heard of, so the entire week leading up to the party turned into a money machine and gave the staff a reason for behaving like kids. Eventually, you like everyone else got sucked along.
Work had hired a big old elegant concert hall that held hundreds and you almost didn't attend when you heard that all the offices north of Manchester would be attending. You simply could not bear to face that many people. However, Charlotte talked you into going over a coffee on a break the next day after her sudden exit, your heart missed a beat every time she told you to make sure you were going to be there. The day previous or the weekend's events were never mentioned again.
You were sure she was just being friendly when she asked, but deep down you really hoped that she meant it.

"Please, please let this be an invite." A voice inside your head kept saying over and over again. You began to dream and imagine what it would be like if she really did want you to go? It could be the greatest day of your life, what if she asked you to be her date? Highly unlikely you knew, but just what if?

The night finally came around and you played it very low key with your costume, dressed in all black you got your next door neighbor to draw a black spider on your left cheek. No reason why a spider and you had no idea what you were supposed to be, your costume was simple and very nondescript, just like you.

"So, what are you supposed to be?" asked Johnny as you walked through the concert hall doors on your own. Faced with a challenge and risk of humiliation right from the off.

"Hmm the spirit of Halloween" you replied, stammering a little as you walked past him and into the main lobby, despite being a little startled at the speed of your sarcasm and comeback.

Johnny was an arsehole from the team next to yours, notorious for liking the sound of his own voice and always centre of attention, but he was always surrounded by females. That night was no exception, even when he was dressed as Pennywise the clown from Stephen King's IT, the shrill of their laughter as he screwed up his face mimicking you before he flicked up his middle finger and pointed directly at your turned back haunted you for the majority of the night and every time you clapped eyes on him at work in the weeks that followed. Still, you had won the first battle, if not the war.

The first time you spotted Charlotte you could physically hear your heart pounding out loud. Stood over by the DJ, her Buffy costume that you had heard so much about and pictured so many times in your head, was there in the flesh for you to marvel at, she looked simply beautiful, even more so than you'd ever imagined.

You stood staring at the young woman that was your first real love, your vision blurred by a dreamlike haze. You watched her, eyes fixated and as you gazed she gave you a little wave. You nearly fell over with shock and undoubted admiration. You had never witnessed the little skips that your heart did right then, tantalizing and invigorating; it would be many years before you felt them again.

The night flew over, the minutes passed with every cheesy song the DJ decided to play next. For fucks sake there was only so many times the Time Warp can be mixed into other tracks before it became as predictable and mundane as your very existence, but you tried your best to enjoy the night and go along with things. Charlotte kept coming over to you to make sure you were ok. That beautiful smile followed by a little dance before she'd trot away back to her friends who were all drinking heavily. She was too, several times you saw her knocking back shots of some putrid green coloured Halloween special spirit. Every time you saw her you felt guilty and intimidated by how easy everybody else seemed to slip into enjoying themselves, it became instantly evident that you quite clearly had no idea of how to have a good time.
Fuck it you thought and headed to the bar, necking back what you had left in your designer bottled lager.
"Two more of these please and a double of that shit" you spat out, beer running down your chin as you pointed towards the big jug of what was labeled up as 'Bulls Testicles' and took pride of place behind the bar.
The bartender was happy to oblige as he took your twenty pound note and didn't give you much change. You turned to face the dancefloor turning your back to the bar, but without leaving the safety of it to lean back on as you downed one bottle of lager. Your eyes were closed as you concentrated on thinking of anything else as you did. Golden and bitter, the Pils flowed quickly down your neck making your eyes water. You paused for a few seconds, already you felt the rush from the sudden intake of alcohol, before you took the next bottle in your hand and flushed that down your neck just as quick.
You let out a little burp, as you quickly blocked your mouth with your sleeve before you checked around to make sure nobody saw or heard! Two down.
Next up the Bulls Testicles. You had no idea what was in it or what it would taste like. Truth be known you will never know as it was quickly down the hatch before you really had a chance to taste it!
The fuzziness was almost instant. Your heart began to race with excitement and as crazy as it sounds, the help from the bull did

give you the effect you were looking for. You looked around that room with a different interpretation after the sudden alcohol infusion. Everyone was having a good time, you had noticed that earlier, even the Ghosts, Ghouls and Zombies, but suddenly you felt part of them, you felt the same as them. You looked again at the costumes dancing by themselves like puppets that had mysteriously came to life. There was Freddie Kruger, there was Jason from Friday the 13th and then you noticed the bull standing in the corner all by himself. He wasn't dancing or fooling around, he was just staring in your direction. He was dressed all in black with horns so big they seemed almost too realistic for the costume, his eyes were simply black too. Black and dead, you couldn't work out if he was staring directly at you or just in your direction? There was something about him you recognized, the feeling of seeing a familiar face in a crowded room full of strangers, but of course you didn't know who was behind the mask. Maybe it was just somebody from your team?

You turned your back on the bull, adrenalin pumped around your body as a new found confidence fuelled by liquor filled your heart and soul. You took one last look at the two empty beer bottles and shot glass on the bar, not giving the familiar horned character in the corner another thought and then you were off. Your body moved like it never had done before as you danced your way towards Charlotte and her friends. Yes, that was you dancing out of time and out of rhythm, but you didn't care. You just wanted to get close to her and as quickly as you could.

Everything else from that point onwards was a blur. You were quickly immersed into the rounds of her and her friends, alcohol flowed with speed and the stimulation made your dancing get a little better.

"One more song before the slow dance!" screamed the DJ as he put his heart and soul into becoming the be all and end all of the ball room. You weren't listening though, Charlotte was coming towards you and whispered something in your ear. You turned to your left desperately trying to hear what she was saying. You closed your eyes and stopped breathing, your concentration was so intense for a slight second that you felt a little sharp pain shoot across your forehead, reaching from one temple to another. She was talking to you, just you and you wanted to capture every word and store it away inside your head forever.

"Let's go outside" she whispered into your ear and without waiting for an answer she grabbed your hand and lead you towards the entrance lobby where Johnny was such a prick on the way in. You were shocked to see he was still there as you reached the exit, still surrounded by girls and still talking shit. Victory was yours though for the night as you noticed the little pause which left his mouth wide open for just a second as he realised exactly who was holding your hand and leading you outside. You won the battle earlier, you had just won the war.

Charlotte said nothing as she led you outside and turned left before quickly turning left again down the back lane that used to lead to the stage door in 'Ball Room' times.

You had no concept of how much the temperature had fallen since you entered just couple of hours ago, but once outside you did. Your heart was racing and all you could focus on was watching the way her hair flowed up and down as she walked, striding and leading you to wherever she planned to take you. Mesmerized, you were totally under her control.

You reached the old stage door and she dropped herself deep into the alcove. Pulling you close you had no time to think about the people who have passed in and out of here in years gone by, instead she was on you, shoving her tongue into your mouth as she grabbed your black shirt by the collar and pulled you closer. You kissed back passionately, you were spellbound. Never before had you felt so much desire and lust. Your hands were everywhere and so were hers. Touching, squeezing, caressing, you both took in every inch of each other's body and savoured every single inch.

You moved your hand under the sash of her leather wooden stake holder that swept across her torso and peeled the fabric from her hot skin before you pushed your hand under the black lacy bra and cup her breast. Flesh on flesh, you were both so aroused that your skin tingled with excitement at every touch. You had never felt like this before, never been so aroused and then she unfastened your belt and un-popped the buttons on your jeans. Taking your fully erect penis in her hands she pulled you closer, lifting her skirt as she did.

You pulled back for a second, looking her straight in the eyes. Your heart was screaming love and lust and emotions that you honestly didn't think existed.

"Take me." She said and pulled you closer. You were now as close as you could ever get to her and she let out a little smile before she pushed you inside her. Both of you gave out a little puff of breath as you realised what had happened, before moving your bodies in tandem and rhythm with each other.

You didn't last very long, quickly pulling out and ejaculating over the hem of her skirt and down those sexy leather boots. The energy that had just been sucked from you forced you to collapse into her arms. You wish you could have stayed there forever.

You shared a taxi home, dropping her off first, but all the way back neither of you really spoke. She cuddled into you, resting her head on your shoulder and wrapping her arms around your waist. When she got out of the cab she gave you a little kiss that started as a peck on the cheek but quickly evolved into something between a little kiss and almost a snog.

Once she has left your chariot you asked the driver to wait as you watched her make her way to the front door of her parent's house. Again, you were fixated as you tried to memorise exactly how she looked as she winded her way up the garden path. She stopped for a second and reached into her handbag for her key. Opening the door, she turned and gave you a little wave. You couldn't be sure because it was dark, but you think she blew you a little kiss, although that may have just been wishful thinking. Then she turned and walked indoors, closing the door behind her and on you. Then she was gone. Happy Halloween.

You never saw Charlotte again. She called in sick for work the next day, then it was the weekend, then you heard she'd been moved to another team in a separate building. You never knew why that happened, at that point in your life that party was the pinnacle, the greatest day of your life, but as quickly as it had happened it was gone forever.

You learnt a valuable lesson in life that Halloween. People come and go in your life, relationships are created and broken, but you can never fully trust anybody, it's the ones that you let into your heart, the ones you love the deepest that leave the biggest scar.

ADOLESCENCE

That night with Charlotte changed your life forever. It started the transformation from child to man and like a caterpillar turning into the winged beauty it would eventually become; you blossomed in your new found maturity. Never quite making the change to a striking butterfly, you were more a hardworking nocturnal moth, less glamorous and divinely attracted to the darkness and bright lights. You were there to serve a purpose.

You never saw Charlotte again, once you thought you did across a crowded bar washed in neon light, but by the time you approached the dance floor she had gone, if of course it really was her. You were never really sure what you would say to her if you ever did see her again, but maybe "Thank you" was all that was needed. She had given you so much more than a knee trembler, she had breathed life into you that night, she had made you come alive.

In the immediate weeks after that Halloween and especially over the Christmas period, you wondered why she had left you so suddenly when the romance had just begun. You wondered if that night had meant as much to her as it had to you. You came up with all kinds of reasons, but deep down you knew the truth. Charlotte was embarrassed about what she had done. Embarrassed, regretful and ashamed. She was so cool at work, the latest fashions, older boyfriends and beautiful. You on the other hand were nobody, not quite the office nerd but not far off. How could she possibly face everyone knowing what she had done that night, knowing who she had fucked down a back alley on a works night out.

The realisation of that though, despite keeping it hidden and never fully admitting it to yourself, seemed to make you grow. You were never going to be used by anyone and let that happen to you again.

The new found determination not to be walked over made you a more outgoing person. Your confidence grew, so much so that as a result you began to be the true you, as if losing that noose around your neck called virginity eased an unbelievable pressure. Which of course it did. You started to talk to people more, both at work and socially, subjects of conversation stopped being a mountain to climb and eventually people started to talk to you.

From small acorns mighty oaks do grow, with your new outgoing personality shining through, you began being invited along on nights out. A little group of you at work began to form into a drinking school, your world became a bigger place and with that you saw places and beautiful people you never thought you'd see. That was the one thing that really came as a shock to you, the beautiful and shiny happy people that had previously only existed in tv shows or the movies. Both male and female specimens draped in the latest trends of fashion, but it was especially the angelic women that caught your attention and became an obsession. Heroes from the screen reproduced in real life and now here you were standing in the same bars as them, rubbing shoulders with them, on occasions even getting to talk to them. Sometimes when you had had enough to drink, you may even try to chat them up.

Such confidence and prowess were a massive turnaround for the shyness and paranoia that had ruled the roost in your life so far. The shackles were well and truly off, meaning your life was a better existence because of it.

Some nights some of the guys got lucky, sometimes they didn't. Still the fun was in the trying. The chase itself was the attraction and human nature made that attraction a competition between you all.

As in any race there was always a favourite, a stallion that usually won more than he lost. In this case the most noble steed was Rob from the accounts department. Six foot plus with a muscular figure that he seemed to do very little with. No need to go to the gym he was just that shape.

Rob was always a hit with the ladies, but never invited them back for seconds. His rule was 'never go back' and at times you felt sorry for the star struck beauty on his arm as she listened to him agree to see her again, when you knew he wouldn't. He never did, and you often thought about how that girl must feel the next day or the next week when the phone never rang. Never go back.

Although maybe that was in fact where you were going wrong? You were a born worrier and you spent too much time worrying and thinking too much about the belle you had just taken advantage of. You were too considerate, but that was how you had been brought up, to respect others. Now in the competition which had become an obsession, everything you had been taught was working against you. You were losing the game by scoring the biggest own goal.

Your success rate was nowhere near as prolific as Rob's, but you did ok. In football terms you'd have finished mid table, a feat you were proud of all things given.

The Five O'clock club after work stretched to most nights, the numbers swelled as you met for Carling in the Black Bull across from the business park. Those nights became weekends, the weekends became fortnights abroad as your list of conquests grew. Rob of course was always streets ahead, but you enjoyed carrying out your work in his shadows. His rich pickings left plenty for you and the rest of the group as those drunken memories blurred into one huge night out. You drank, got drunk and fucked. Then you did it over and over again.

Far too much fun and happiness for here, that isn't the reason we are telling this story…..

KNOCKED SENSELESS

It was on one of those notorious nights out that you nearly lost your life for the first time. It had been a pretty wild one, beginning at twelve in the afternoon to catch the Saturday football and continuing well into the early hours finishing just in time for the Sunday morning football.

Although you had certainly enjoyed yourself and made the most of the rare Saturday off work, it had been a fruitless expedition in terms of finding female company to escort you home. Instead you found yourself standing alone in the greasy kebab shop waiting for 'cheesy chips' and garlic sauce. A pathetic dish of fried potatoes covered in mass produced rubbery grated cheese. The piece de resistance being the thick salad cream like garlic sauce poured all over the top, so it slops down the side of the pale yellow polystyrene container, dribbling onto your hands as the 'chef' hands it over to you. Disgusting in substance, in preparation and in taste, but at two thirty in the morning after fourteen and a half hours drinking you genuinely couldn't think of anything more appetising to defeat the demon that was the hunger in your stomach. Stodge was what your body craved, and stodge was certainly what it was going to get.

Before that though, before your hands got polluted by cheap and cheerful junk food spilling down their sides, you used the ten minutes of waiting in the queue to observe your surroundings and look at the other beings of the night that shared such a grubby setting.

The kebab shop at that time of the morning was nothing but a den of iniquity. People coming and going, some so drunk that they have to focus to simply put one foot in front of the other never mind decide what they want to eat. However, once they are there and been served they are completely focused on carrying their pizza home. Handling it as if it was the Turin Shroud, they will make it all the way home without dropping a slice, before they fall asleep head first in the cardboard box and waking later that morning with mushed tomato puree and thin strands of cheese hanging off their faces. They are the happy ones, simple and happy.

Then there's the people who shouldn't have been there. The ones whose partners thought they were somewhere else, away with the lads, out with the girls or perhaps the worst of all, out on a works night out.

These are the ones that were there with people they shouldn't be. Illicit affairs because they were all so saddened by what they had. Saddened and frightened to change it, or maybe they were just unable to see beyond what they already had and thus unable to change it. Is the grass ever greener? Easy to spot as they were wrapped round each other like cheap Packa Macs. Clinging on for dear life, frightened to let each other go as that would mean returning to the mundane reality of their unhappy existence. Home, work, marriage, children. Right there in that kebab shop they were free and with someone they didn't really give a fuck about. Free to kiss in public and grope indecently, free to show excitement, arousal and a seedy desire to be cheap and sexy. At two thirty in the morning everything else they have in their boring lives didn't exist, they were there with whoever and the food they were wasting their time ordering is simply a way of extending the night. It's only a matter of time and where they will end up fucking a strangers brains out. It could have been the back alley around the corner from the kebab shop, the back of the taxi after which they got dropped off two streets away from home, or maybe even back at a friend's house. One thing was certain those people would be screwing tonight, whilst their other halves were at home in bed alone, shattered after a stressful night looking after the kids.

The world has done a full circle for these people. They were once the sexy, horny people who were not afraid to express themselves and were up for screwing everything and everywhere. The world has turned and that night they were stuck at home whilst their partners were out doing the same as they both did when they met. Yet next weekend it will be their turn and they intend to make the time away count. That was just how fucked up the lives of those people had become.

Then there were the opposites, poles apart but still not on their own unlike you. These couples don't talk. Not to each other, not to anyone else in waiting for such delicacies, even ordering their food is like appearing on an episode of Mastermind despite being the exact same order that they have ordered for the last twenty years that they have been together.

No contact with each other, no holding hands or hugging, he stood with his hands in his pockets as she grasped her handbag as if it was made of gold. Desperate to hide it from the prying eyes of everyone present, although everyone else is too busy preoccupied with their own deviancy to have noticed her priceless treasure.

It was you and the others like you that she was particularly concerned about, the ones there in solitude. She may be extremely unhappy in her marriage and living out the same Saturday night for the last twenty years but at least she wasn't alone. You were; thus, her conditioned mind can't understand how you could have lived like that. Human nature makes things that are different something to be afraid of. She was afraid of you, afraid and nervous.

Standing there with a gaze far off and distant as you tried to focus on the menu and all the exotic choices it held, you knew you would just order what you always did, still this way you didn't look as sad, you didn't look as if this was what you did every Saturday night, order food for one.

You weren't actually alone though, there were more and more just like you arriving by the minute. Some more drunk than others, some splattered with blood from the fist fight they had in the last bar which resulted in them being ejected and losing their mates. Ending up here was almost like displaying the trophy. Yes, they are on their own but 'you should have seen the other guy.'

All you singletons know your night could have been so different and as you tried to comprehend where your night took the path that lead to loneliness, the queue moved down, the people move on. Move on to fuck, move on to separate rooms, move on to sleep on a mate's couch or even the floor in the hall as they just made it through the door before collapsing head first into a drink induced coma.

The garlic sauce ran down your fingers as you turned right outside and head to where you thought you may manage to get a taxi. You hadn't noticed how cold the night had become when you'd stepped in and ordered food, but now you've been in the warm and come back outside goose pimples developed on your bare arms, suddenly just a t shirt didn't seem such a good idea!

You walked and ate, ate and walked, throwing a hand out to every vehicle that happened to drive by you in the hope it could be your chariot home. It doesn't matter whether it has a vacant yellow light or even if it is a car, the fuzz that was the very little sober part of your brain told you to stick your hand in the air every time you saw a set of headlights approach. Of course, none of them stopped.

You had a little chuckle to yourself as you pictured what you must have looked like to the passing motorists. A Sunday league linesman sprung to mind, throwing your arm in the air every time the opposition pushed forward, or in this case every time a vehicle draws close, "Offside!" you shouted at the next three cars that passed. None of which stopped, neither did your laughing. Drunks can find the simplest of things amusing.

Eventually the smile subsided, as it began to dawn on you that unless you could come up with a master plan you were going to have walk the whole ten miles home. Suddenly your heart sank, and the linesman gag didn't seem as funny anymore. You needed a fucking lift home!

First though you needed to relieve the nagging desire to urinate that had crept up on you like a hunting leopard from behind, a natural predator stalking its prey. You had subconsciously been trying to ignore it for about the last ten minutes or so, but as you scoffed the last handful of grated cheese and garlic sauce into your mouth, the chips were finished a long time ago, you realised that you couldn't refuse any longer.

Standing next to a rectangular stone bin you forgot all the manners your mother taught you as you licked whatever was left out of the yellow carton, squeezing your eyes shut as you fight against the horrible feeling the polystyrene left on your tongue and teeth, then you threw it into the bin. Those chips meant everything to you not that long ago but now they've gone they meant nothing, consumed and then worthless, what had been so vital now meant absolutely fuck all. The emphasis has shifted to something else. At that moment in time your bladder took priority, you needed to piss and nothing else mattered.

You set off again, running your fingers through the leaves from the plants in the concrete planters that act as the middle man between two lines of high street shops, as you tried to remove the grease from your fingers. Everywhere you looked in your desperate search for a place to toilet there were security cameras staring back at you. Big Brother watched your every move and that made you feel very uneasy. The fact that somebody could have been observing your movements, behavior and actions made you feel very self conscious. Who was watching? Was it security? Was it the Police? Was it the dubious mob that ran the country, the Government? What if it was the bull from your dreams?

You found a little cut between two shops and darted down it thinking the moment for relief had arrived. You were just undoing your belt, so your desperate clumsy fingers could start to undo the metal buttons on your jeans when headlights shone towards you from the other end of the cut. They swept a full circumference, lighting up the alley you were standing in and the whole world, as they pulled in to turn around. Whilst they didn't appear to see you, the fluorescent stripes along the side of the car were enough for you to know that it wasn't the time to take a leak. Fastening your belt as you moved, you began to run back the way you came, hitting the main shopping street you continued to run. Some new found freedom from this little spurt of energy kept you moving and also distracted you from your full bladder that was sloshing around in your loins as your designer shoes pounded on the paving slabs.

The sudden burst of energy and clarity had an almost sobering effect on you and, as your pace slowed you checked over your shoulder and nodded your approval that no police car had followed you nor an officer on foot for that matter. You began to relax.

Your pace slowed even further and with the grace of a buzzard gliding in the wind before resting on his perch, so he could survey his land and of course his prey, you came to a standstill. The chill of earlier had disappeared, replaced with a warmth and stickiness produced by the adrenalin and sweat clinging your clothes to your body from your getaway.

Relaxed a little more, the chill may have gone but the chronic ache in your bladder had returned with a vengeance. You glanced left then right, just a group of people a couple of hundred yards away. Far enough you thought and with that you ducked down

another back lane between an electrical shop and a bakers. You headed to the very far end of the alley and saw the back door way to the electrical shop on your right. You knew it wasn't really the right thing to do, but needs must and for the second time that night you undid your belt without female company. This time though, you went a step further and managed to unfasten the brushed metal buttons of your jeans. You finally turned on the tap, the relief as urine splashed up against the shop doorway was orgasmic, as steam rose from the pavement which created a tiny smoke screen like something from a minute horror film. Something bad could have been lurking behind that steam.
Relieving yourself seemed to go on forever and you found yourself wondering how your body could have held onto so much liquid as the pressure finally began to subside from your bladder.
You were just fastening yourself back up when you heard voices coming into the alleyway. You panicked and caught your foreskin in one of the buttons, letting out a little shriek and almost jumping out of the sanctuary of your doorway where you would have been in full view of whoever was descending. The voices were coming nearer but they didn't seem to have heard you injuring yourself in a very delicate place. They just kept coming.
You stood completely still, hidden by the alcove of the doorway. Safety in hiding you thought, listening you could make out several different voices, maybe three or four males, all with accents. Then catching you by surprise you heard another voice, a higher pitched and more fragile voice, the voice of a woman and she sounded as if she was distressed and frightened. You peered around the corner of your hiding place and focused on the group just twenty yards away.
Four Asian men were standing around one blonde female. One man had pulled her skimpy top off her shoulders and revealed a black silky bra with lace around the edge of the cups, two others then pushed her against the wall with each one forcing her back by each shoulder. The fourth man had pushed his hand up her red leather mini skirt. She kicked out trying to get them off her but there were too many of them and they were too strong. One of her matching red stilettos flew across the alley floor as she aimed

another desperate kick at the youth who had now forced his fingers into her vagina.

You knew you had to do something to make this stop and without weighing up the odds of four against one, or thinking about the consequences you stepped out from behind the safety of the doorway that had served so well as your own personal toilet. Having left the seclusion of your secret place you were now an easy target, but you knew you couldn't have let this go on.

"Oi! What are you doing" you shouted puffing out your chest to make you look bigger than you actually were. You didn't do this deliberately; it was just part of your body's natural defence system and a very manly gesture!

The four men stopped still in their tracks and all turned to face you in unison. How dare somebody attempt to stop them from their gang rape? Who would have had the audacity to do such a thing?

"You gonna make me white boy?" said the one doing the molesting as he pulled his hand out of the girl and started walking towards you, running his fingers under his nose and smelling her as he did. An inflammatory gesture if there ever was one, as well as being a little perverted!

The one who was leading the undressing followed just a pace behind him and all of a sudden you were face to face with the pair of rapists.

Deep hazelnut eyes stared into yours, intimidating and threatening, making that chest of yours shrink back into itself.

"Fuck" you said under your breath. Glancing over the shoulder of the assailants in front of you, you saw that only one of the men was holding the girl now. The other had begun to make his way to join his friends in front of you. He too had come to see who had had the cheek to stop his fun. Three against one, you were seriously outnumbered.

"Just think you should leave her alone, that's all" you stammered. "There's four of you and she really doesn't seem to want play."

With that the 'leader of the gang' took a stride forward. His nose almost touched yours as he leaned right into you.

"Maybe we should play with you instead?" he laughed out loud, then with a motion so quick you didn't even see it coming, he slammed his forehead into your nose sending stars and flashes right through your senses and across your forehead. Blood filled your vision as your nose exploded, the pain shot across your temples and up onto your brain. Your knees trembled both with shock and the blow, stunned and dazed, then before you knew it you were on the ground, defeated before it had begun.

Time stood still for a brief second as you lay there unable to fully comprehend what had just happened. You could hear the voices above chattering excitedly in some foreign tongue you didn't understand, then the blows began. One size 8 loafer to the side of your head, a sharp needle like pain shot through your temple once more, the pain overlaying the original one. Then another boot to the front of your head, such force and hatred, your nose smashed even further across your face. Your eyes filled up with blood again and as the third blow came in the shape of a stamp on top of the head, the last thing you remembered was the noise and pain of a front tooth losing its battle with the concrete below, causing you permanent disfigurement and loss.

When you came around daylight was just beginning to show its face. Almost resentfully it seemed, but there is no doubt the darkness of the night before was subsiding and reluctantly giving way to a new start. Your mouth was full of dried blood and bits of broken tooth, both of which contributed towards the stale metallic taste that flooded your mouth. Opening your eyes fully you saw nothing else but blood, your blood, dried now but having formed a fluid balloon shape around your head. Every inch of your body ached and the sharp pain that shot across your broken ribs as you tried to push you self up onto all fours, was enough to make you give up after one attempt.

You sank back down to the sad and helpless position in which you regained consciousness, you were totally fucked. There was no sign of your attackers and perhaps more ironically there was no sign of the beautiful blonde damsel in distress. You could have dreamt it all if it wasn't for the intoxicating pain that riddled its way all through your body. Where was she? Where had everyone gone? It was as if all this has been for nothing. All that was left to prove that the battle had actually existed was one red stiletto shoe just a few feet away from where you had just regained consciousness. The heel broken in two, ironic as your body felt that way also, from where you too had been repeatedly hammered off the concrete.

With that thought you sank your head back onto the pavement below, in agony and defeated.

You had no idea of how long had passed before you were found by the electrical shop manager as he stepped over you on his way to open the back door, but when his appearance woke you from another weary slumber, you knew that your injuries meant serious medical attention was needed and quickly.

However, you couldn't move. You were paralysed by pain, silent and broken you lay there motionless until you heard the keys jangle as he took them from a pocket of his pin striped suit and after carefully selecting the correct one, you heard the turn of the lock and the door open. Unaware he wasn't alone, you got a little shock as he stopped before entering through your substitute toilet.

"I'll put the lights on Barbara, you call an ambulance."

LOVE SONG

The first time you met her you knew she was the one for you. Your eyes caught sight of that beautiful woman, fixed your vision right onto her like a tracking beam, instantly you could feel your pulse begin to work overtime. Slowly at first, your heart began to beat faster, then faster, then faster. From the minute your gaze was glued on this wonderful creation, your brain knew that your life had just changed forever. She was the one for you.

You watched as she moved, completely in love with the way her body swayed back and forth as she walked and the way her long dark red hair flowed behind her, mimicking her body's movements just fraction of a second behind the rhythm.

The sun shone down on her like a halo that day, as it used its own soft golden rays to reflect glistening strands of crimson, purple and deep magenta. Beauty in person, perfection in human form, everything you ever wanted.

She was the one for you, of that you had no doubt. Your heart melted that day and still does whenever you think of her, even though you have erased the finer details like where and when from your memory to ease the pain of later.

A love so deep it hurts to believe it, a love so pure and determined you couldn't beat it. Even if you had wanted to, nothing could make it be better than how she made you feel, nothing on earth could be more natural.

She was a couple of years younger than you, but it didn't seem to matter. Age had no place in a love like that, you were made for each other, meant to be from the moment you were both born. That's all that mattered; you were together like you were supposed to be, peas in a pod, soul mates, together forever, like it was meant to be.

There was a song playing on the radio that moment you met her, a love song that you have also erased from your memory for your own personal protection. Words that meant so much back then but would go on to hurt even harder, words that provided the perfect backdrop for love at first sight. That song never left you and always reminded you of her, deep down you hoped it reminded her of you too.

Funny how someone else's words can mean so much to somebody else, as if they'd been written so very deliberately just for you and her. Your song, a love song.

The days after that first meeting were like a whirlwind of happiness and fun. You talked and laughed either on the phone or in person several times per day, constantly in touch, neither of you ever got bored or ran out of things to say, there were never any difficult silences during the conversations and there was never a moment that either of you were too busy for the other, perfect harmony in two beings.

The sex came soon into the relationship because the burning passion and desire just made it too difficult to resist. An animal attraction that had brought you together and matched the intellectual connection that also glued your hearts together. Your bodies fitted each other perfectly and the result was the best love making you had ever experienced. Hot, regular and whenever the desire took over, you loved every second you were intimately connected together, you loved exploring her and finding out what made her happy, what she liked and of course what made her cum.

Every time you heard that song it got you in the mood and sometimes you would just stick it on the cd player just to get her in the mood. She never took much persuading though. You were so connected, nothing could stop this. This was so right, nothing would ever come between you, you loved her too much and you thought she felt the same about you.

It wasn't long before you moved in together, enabling you to spend more time together and as the bond grew stronger, you became even closer. She sold her little flat in the city and moved into your bigger semi detached on the out skirts. The money from the sale of her place helped you live a life that was pleasurable without being excessive, a life that was full but not over the top.

Holidays abroad at least three times a year and meals out at least three times a week. It was heavy laden with self indulgence but not ridiculous, satisfying without becoming laborious, the excitement never ceased and the loved continued to grow.

You were made for each other, of that you were sure, plus you were as sure as you could be that she felt that way too. The perfect match that you'd been longing for all your life, the dream of a woman and man being united by their desire for each other, you never imagined you could be this happy.

Eventually you decided to sell your place too, move away from city life and concentrate on the simpler things in life, like being together and starting a family. You promised each other that work was there to help you live, you didn't live to work. The move would give you more time for each other and take away all the distractions of the day to day lives that you currently owned. Nothing could stop you or the fantasy you were living, there could be nothing that would ever come between you.

Life has a really wicked sense of humor though, a habit of not playing the game that you think you are, so, despite trying everything, the baby didn't come. You practiced every trick in the book and tried every old wife's tale, but nothing ever happened. The continuation and heir to your thrown just never arrived and whilst it upset you it never affected you the way it did her, you certainly didn't blame her or love her any less.

In fact, the failure to reproduce made you love her more and gave you the burning ambition to make her truly happy. You got on with life and enjoyed the trying, but deep down you knew she was really hurting. You started to blame yourself, but you were doing all you could. What else could you do?

It was about then the bull used to appear every night in your dreams, it was as if he preyed on weakness.

Not actually doing anything, not causing you any need to worry, he would simply just appear and let you know that he was around. Usually after you'd just had sex and lay there afterwards with your whole body shaking as you wondered if that was the time that would change your lives forever?

It was impossible not to relax and doze into some sort of euphoric sleep, contented, that was when he would come. It was as if he was watching and waiting, ready to suck and take all the happiness away, but he never did. He stayed detached, on the peripheral, outside looking in, but you were always too busy buzzing from your orgasm to really notice.

Her job started going really well, which you were both pleased about. She was doing so well that even with the disappointment of not conceiving, promotion seemed to follow promotion.

You were proud of her, but also a little jealous, as you had seemed to have reached your level in your own career with nowhere upwards to move too.

Still you were pleased for her and it was a bitter sweet moment when she came home and told you that she had been successful in another promotion application, only this now meant she was earning more money than you. Bringing home a larger slice of the family crust, she was now number one, the breadwinner.
It hurt but you just got on and accepted it. You both loved each other so much, did it really matter who earned the most?
You had your dream home; your dream life and you had her. Your heart still sang every time you saw her and when you opened your eyes each morning you had the exact same feeling that you did the very first time you saw her, when that song was playing on the radio.
You loved her so much that nothing could possibly stop the devotion you shared, nothing could come between you, ever.
You quickly got over the hurt of the male ego and actually became accustomed to being a kept man. It didn't affect your relationship or lifestyle, in fact it enriched it. The holidays got more exotic, as the evening's wine got more expensive. Sharing bottles after work and talking about the days you had both encountered, gave you a reason to get up in the morning and a reason to go home at night.
You lived for those evenings, perfection and happiness beyond your wildest dreams, you never thought you could feel this way about anyone or that anyone would ever feel this way about you.
Always in the background there was that song that you heard that first night. The love song that played as you fell in love in an instant. Love at first sight, the love song that meant so much to you then and always will.
Your days together grew bigger and better than you ever believed possible, like something from a Hollywood movie. As you grew together and became one, the love was so strong, nothing could possibly tear you apart.

WINTER

The temperature dropped like a stone, every year it did the same thing, every year you complained about it, but could do nothing. It was no exception this time around, but this year you were determined to be prepared for it, accept it and perhaps more importantly, survive.

Then the temperature plummeted, so you complained, you moaned, in fact it hit you even harder because you'd built yourself up into a false security that you could handle it and deal with whatever forces Mother Nature through at you, when the truth was that you couldn't really deal with much.

"Light a fire baby" she said as you helped her through the front door, her hands full of shopping bags. You smiled, contented that she was back with you, you always felt happier when she was home safe and there was just the two of you. You loved her so much.

"Sure. I've literally just got in too." You said taking four carrier bags out of her hands and placing them on the kitchen bench.

"Is there any more?"

"Nope, that's all I could afford until payday on Friday." She said pulling a sad face. Finances were so hard back then as you battled to afford your dream home, but together you were strong, you knew you would pull through.

You'd just recently accepted responsibility for where you were in your life, finally you had decided to pull yourself out of the rut you were in at work and applied for a position that was a couple of grades above your current role. With the job came extra responsibility, but the increased salary would make it worthwhile, as well as more than trebling your input into the family pot.

You gave her a little kiss on the end of her nose to reassure her that everything was going to be ok and she gave you a little smile in return.

"I'll go put that fire on. You go put your feet up for five."

Her smile becomes wider and without moving from the porch unzips her fake fur lined boots before taking it in turn to use the toes of each foot to kick the boot off. Positioning them in front of the radiator in the passage to dry off and also warm up the following morning, she goes and collapses onto the sofa, coat and scarf still on. You loved the way she did that. She always looked so cute when she engulfed herself into a heaven of blankets and cushions. Simply beautiful you thought, as you glanced over your shoulder whilst on bended knee as you strategically positioned the kindling and the fire lighters. Blowing on the smoldering twigs, the fire catches quite easily. She was so tired and enjoying relaxing on the sofa with her eyes shut that she didn't notice you stand up or leave the room. She was happy to be home and you were happy she was there.

When you returned though carrying a bag of logs that you spent all day Sunday cutting and a glass of freshly poured Cabernet Sauvignon, she greeted you with another smile, this time one of contentment.

Outside the blizzard began, as the wind began to pick up, howling its way around your little cottage, blowing tiny flakes of snow in every direction. The wind was strong and forceful, it was as if it was trying to get in to blow you around too.

The kindling had fully taken by then and as you threw the first of the evenings many logs on the fire, you too began to relax. Slouched against the sofa, you started to have those hazy memories that you have when you were so relaxed that your brain finally forgot everything that had haunted it all day. Lighting the fire was always a special moment in your eyes, such a natural way to keep warm, you had been fascinated by a naked flame flickering since you were a child.

When you were about five years old your family visited a relative's home and after afternoon tea you retreated to the sitting room to 'catch up.' In reality the men would fall asleep in front of a roaring fire whilst the woman chatted about all the latest gossip, news you were too young to understand or to follow, but your mind was always elsewhere anyway.

The flames danced in front of you, changing hue from yellow to orange to red as you looked on, the embers crackling was a sound you had never heard before, it was like the flames had a story to tell but only if you listened carefully enough. Maybe they were trying to pass on a message, maybe they were trying to tell you your future? Either way that Sunday afternoon you listened. You were the only one that listened, you were the only one that heard what they had to say

The kindling had done well, whilst the flames were roaring through the first log, she slumped back into the sofa, wine glass

in hand as she loosened her scarf with the other. Happy she was sorted you stood and left the room again to go and pour yourself a glass of wine, then you could sit next to her and cuddle in.
"The forecast says the snow is in for the night." She shouted through to you, flicking the flakes of snow from her coat and watching them melt into the carpet one by one, one of nature's miracles gone forever with that one simple flick.
"Maybe you could bring some more wood in?"
"Sure, leave all that to me, you've had a hard day at work." You smiled to yourself at that moment because you loved her so much and seeing her warm and comfy like she was made you feel good in yourself, it gave you a purpose and a meaning. You couldn't have asked for anymore.
The wind howled as the snow fell faster and thicker as you both sat down to tea. The fire was crackling away, but you weren't listening this time, instead with it getting colder and colder you resisted the opportunity to set the dinner table and succumbed to the temptation of eating off trays in front of the wall of warmth. A truly personal, cozy and sexual moment all at once, a special memory of how life was.
She was warmer now and had taken off her coat to reveal a little off the shoulder woolen jumper, her cheeks were rosy with heat and as she tucked into her meal you gazed in awe at her beauty. You really did love her with all your heart. The glow radiating from her body's warmth was the most beautiful thing that you had ever seen, you cuddled in, sharing the heat.
Outside there was the clatter of plant pots falling off stands, but you didn't hear them due to the swirling of the blizzard rattling around the garden, looking through the French doors everything was white, everything was cold.
The 'whoosh' of the swirling wind blowing and dancing outside the safety of the double glazing created a melancholy atmosphere inside, but outside the snow storm was really gathering pace as it became dangerous. Far off across the fields and down the hills you could see the headlights of cars containing people trying to get from A to B when really, they should have just stayed at A. They moved at a snail's pace and as you glanced up from the comfort of your sofa you couldn't help feeling that the white stuff falling from the sky was some kind of magic spell that was

making the whole world run in slow motion. The whole world except your sitting room, inside there with just you two, a different magic was happening, the power of love.

She had now begun to relax into a more chilled mental state as her body began to leave the chills behind and instead became taken over by the red hot heat of the fire. You were both snuggled on the sofa, silent but content. Holding her wine glass in her right hand, she weaved her left one under your arm and held your waist pulling you closer. Two people in love, two people keeping each other warm, two people keeping each other safe.

THE FALL

ANGER

Today was never supposed to be like this, for fucks sake you just rose to go to work like any other day, but that was where you made your first mistake, opening your eyes and giving the go ahead to a new day. Let the games commence.

You were still bleary eyed when you ventured out of the safety and comfort of the bedroom and down the hall in your dressing gown, tying the belt around your waist as you pass through the sitting room and open the door into the kitchen.

You do a slight detour once entering, taking a left instead of going straight ahead towards the door of the utility room where the dogs sleep. With one thing in mind you pass around the kitchen table, tapping your fingers off the back of all four seats as you go, your gaze fixed on the Tassimo coffee machine. It is already filled with water and placing the Espresso pod in the jaws of the beast was the last thing you did before venturing to the sanctuary of bed last night.

All you need to do is push your finger against the on/off switch.

A simple task, but as you lean forward to do so the baggy sleeve of your grey terry towline dressing gown catches one of the small glass coffee cups that you placed last night, his and hers, cleaned and ready for the caffeine rush you are desperate for every morning.

The glass tumbles, bouncing not once but twice on the wooden floor, you hold your breath, maybe it will make it....

Of course, it doesn't, and you can only stand there as it shatters into a million pieces right before your eyes. You once had a set of four, but like everything else in your life your collection has began to fall apart. This morning's escapade means you are now down to the last one. For fucks sake, not much good when you need to make two.

Putting the dustpan and brush back in the cupboard that they call home after emptying its contents into the bin, you turn back towards the cupboard above where the mugs are kept. You need that caffeine fix even more now, despite it still only being 6.30am. How are you going to be able to get through today? You take a deep breath and continue on.

After finally completing the mundane task of making two espresso's you take one back to the bedroom where she is sleeping. She is snoring and even though you kiss her forehead and tap her shoulders, she does not stir. If only she knew what you'd been through already to make them.

Leaving the bedroom, you pick your own small drink up in the oversized mug, as you pass through the kitchen to go and see the dogs in the utility. Swigging the coffee down in one go and place the mug on the bench next to the sink. You open the door to the utility room and suddenly the strong smell of coffee is replaced by an equally overpowering odor of one of the dogs having a severely upset stomach. Before you can even reach the window to let some fresh air in, or before your eyes even have the chance to focus on where the mess is, you feel a squelch under your slipper as you foot slides away from you!

It still isn't even 7am yet.

After another clean up job of both the utility room and your slipper, you get ready for work quietly, before you make your escape leaving her to enjoy a lie in on a rare day off.

You have never really enjoyed the drive to work, not necessarily just this job, but every job you've ever had. Mainly because you are nearly always running late, adding pressure to your brain as it constantly seems to tell you where you should be at that particular time, or how far along you'd be on a normal day.

The pressure brings anxiety, as human nature kicks in and your head and heart fill with negative feelings. Today is no exception, but this morning you have also had to contend with the clean up mission in both the kitchen and the utility.

You can still smell the deep chestnut smell of dog shit, but also you can still feel the slide under your foot, the worry for your balance, plus the cold feeling of waste expired of any use to the canine body through the plastic as you peeled it off the tiled floor and bagged it up using four bags!

Even the fact you are having these thoughts instead of concentrating on your driving shows just how trivial your day to day life has become. Nobody else on this road will be driving along right now thinking about dog shit and how many bags it took to clean it up. No, every other driver will be planning for the day ahead, practicing what they are going to say in that important meeting, working on a plan to clinch that life changing deal or looking forward to a secret dinner date with their secretary. You laugh out loud at the thought of that one, the laughter producing a very rare moment indeed.

Why the fuck has she just pulled out in front of you? She was just sitting there at that junction, neither looking right nor left, just sitting there and then she pulled out. You slam your brakes on and quickly look in your rear view mirror, bracing yourself for another car or something even bigger ploughing into the back of you. There is nothing, time itself has saved your life, luck would have it that at that very second you were in the only vehicle on the road.

Yet still she pulled out in front of you, her brand new and faceless little 'micro' car that probably has an engine size similar to your Dyson vacuum cleaner, she was never going to be able to accelerate away once she was on the road. Why couldn't she have just waited until you got passed?

You smack your palm off the centre piece of the steering wheel making the horn set of a squeal that could wake the dead, and as the road leaves behind the street lights of the little hamlet you are passing through, a man stirs in his bed and looks at his watch. He is awake early, awake and annoyed. He looks at his watch again as he slumps his head back onto his pillow, he is awake early because of your car horn and now his day has gotten off to not the start he wanted. Maybe his morning will pan out something like yours.

The road winds away from the man and the small collection of houses that surround him. The sun still isn't fully awake yet either and all you can see in the dusky light is the black walls of hedges that form the boundary to your way out. Black hedges and the red glow of the woman's tail lights.

Why the fuck did she have to pull out in front of you? Only she can really say, but you suspect that she doesn't even know herself. Maybe she is oblivious to you the fact that she could have killed you, oblivious to the fact that she even has company on the road this morning.

You reach a small stretch of the road that gets a little wider and out loud you wish for her to pull in, so you can get past. She doesn't of course, despite your harsh toot and it becomes clear that actually she is unaware to your existence and to the fact that you are even there.

The speed limit for this road is 60mph, your new obstruction is ambling along at 30. You can feel yourself filling with rage. Like a bottle under the hot water tap the fury is rising and you start fidgeting in your seat as you urge her to pull over. Leaning forward and crouching over the steering wheel you hope that somehow your new driving position will transmit the urgency of your journey to the nuisance ahead. Little beads of sweat start to form on your brow, instantly erasing that clean and soapy feeling that a fresh morning shower gives you. You begin to perspire more and already you can feel little damp patches forming in the arm pits of your crisp and recently ironed white shirt.
"Fuck" you shout to nobody but yourself, punching the steering wheel as you do.
"Fuck, fuck fuck!" Punching the steering wheel again.
"Get out of the fucking way woman!" But still she doesn't pull to the side to let you by or put her foot a little harder on the accelerator. You glance at your watch as you slam the gearstick down a cog as the woman drops her speed to below 20mph to go around a wide sweeping corner.
"Get out of the way!" You scream again, as she picks up speed gently but peaks again at 30mph.
You are definitely late now, but you try and plan ahead. You need to get past this woman and get yourself back on track. Up in front, about half a mile, there is a little stretch where the road is very straight and a fraction wider. Maybe if there is nothing coming you could get past her there? You shift forward, placing your buttocks on the edge of the driver's seat, urging the road to straighten.
You round a corner that takes the road to the left, the veins in the side of your forehead beginning to pump in anticipation of being able to get past, to move your day forward and maybe, just maybe make up some of the time you've already lost. You sit even straighter knowing you are nearly there, your fingers take a tighter grip on the wheel that steers this ship, your eyes fixed on the road ahead, scouring for obstacles. The way your morning is going you expect to see a big yellow tractor heading your way or a herd of cows being forced along the road by a farmer on a quad dressed all in green, shouting and swearing at the money machines he is moving to pastures new before slaughter.

To your amazement nothing is coming, the road is clear heading towards you, now is your chance.

You block change from fifth gear to second and your engine lets out a screech of both excitement and shock as you jolt the car to the right and out onto the other side of the road at a right angle.

Instantly you are alongside the menace that has held back your day for the last six miles, staring straight at her through your passenger window and her driver's window, you cast a glare that should have turned her to stone.

She just stares ahead at the road, oblivious to you and to the fact that she has even been overtaken. Eyes never flickering from the road ahead and her speed at that annoying 30mph.

Quarter of a mile further on, you take your foot off the accelerator and hit the brake, quickly reducing your speed again as your engine lets out a little sigh of relief. This is your turning onto the motorway, with three lanes of traffic stretching out for miles in front of you. Nothing can stop you now and as you pull out into the middle lane and your speed hits seventy you are finally on your way. Eventually after a start to darken anybody's day, your morning has broken.

You arrive at work fifteen minutes late, which is better than you expected, but thankfully your boss has been called to a manager's meeting, so you are able to slink behind your desk without anyone really noticing. Anyone that is, apart from Andy.

Typical, as you quickly pull your brief case up to your knees with a plan of scattering a load of papers over the desk, so you look a lot busier than you obviously are and as if you have been there a while, you realise that you are not alone.

Clunk goes the metallic unlocking sound of the combination lock of the brief case. Clunk again as you open the other side, but the noise is quickly absorbed by an annoying voice you know all too well.

"Oh! We started a back shift now have we?" smirks Andy, Dr Who coffee cup in his hand which has an annoying chip on the rim, a brown chunk in the white porcelain. Despite the obvious haven for germs Andy will never throw the mug out, Dr Who is his life.

"Erm no, no just problems with traffic." You reply. Your heart wants to declare everything you have been through to even get here, to tell him how grateful he should be that you are actually in, but Andy isn't the person to share that information with. If you let your tongue slip you might as well of paid for a huge advert on the intranet or taken a full page in the company magazine.

"Just trouble with the traffic" you repeat shaking your head, eyes refusing to look at him as you continue to unpack a pile of papers from the brief case that is still perched on your knee.

Andy nods and then makes the most unsubtle glance towards the mundane grey and white clock on the office wall above the cheese plant, which has been in the office so long that it is possibly older than you, just so you know he has definitely taken a mental snap shot of your arrival time. The company robot recording data, useless and annoying data, that is Andy.

Taking a sip from his mug featuring his one obsession in life, he smirks and turns to walk away greeting your manager as he walks back into the office from his meeting, his head clearly full of all of today's targets that have just been rammed into his ears. Is this all you can aspire to be? Is your managers job all you have to aim for? You shake your head again and concentrate back on the pulp in your black leather briefcase.

"Good morning Mr Brown, can I get you a coffee?" he asks, scurrying towards the far corner of the floor space to where Mr Brown is heading to his personal office. Completely oblivious to the lap dog hurrying to catch him up from behind, tongue hanging out and desperate to give him a paw.

"Arsehole!" you mutter under your breath, finally arranging those papers on your desk. It's going to be a long day.

Andy kept an eye on you all day from that morning's discussion. It wasn't his job too, but he obviously felt the need to watch and pass everything back to Mr Brown. It was as if he was almost desperate to trip somebody up. Proving a colleague to be inadequate would intensify the need for him and cement his existence deep into the office walls. Hardly surprising really as he had very little else in his life, you often wondered if Andy's one aim in was to outlive that cheese plant and thus become invincible.

Into his early 30's, Andy had still never left home. Living with his mother only as his father had passed away several years ago after a long battle with dementia. Andy clearly felt his mother needed him and hence he stayed at home. However, in reality it was him that needed his mother.

He had worked for the company since leaving school and had seen many a member of staff come and go in that time, as well as seeing policies and projects change. He'd always stayed though, the one constant and familiar face. Almost as grey in personality and existence as that damned office clock which today was the sword he planned to slay you with. Although harmless really, he was just the type of person to annoy everyone.

Today it was your turn to be made the office scapegoat and come home time you really had had enough of his annoying and immature wise cracks. As the clock struck 5pm you started to pack the same papers back into your brief case, having hardly even looked at them throughout the day, just as Mr Brown left his office to head home after his own stressful day, Andy smirked to himself and looked up from his PC, obviously planning to stay and work a little later unpaid.

"Oh, are you going already? I thought you would have been staying a little later with coming in late this morning?"

You just glare at him as Mr Brown turns and casts you a skeptical look from behind his glasses, but he doesn't stop, he continues to walk away much to Andy's frustration. He too it would appear has had enough of today and this office. You can see the embarrassment of failure sweep across Andy's face, that wasn't the reaction he was hoping for.

"No Andy" you say, "Some of us have lives to get back to" and with a snap of the brief case lock you are standing up and putting your coat on. You don't look back at Andy, you decide that you don't want to give him the satisfaction. Plus, you'd probably punch him if you did.

Outside it is raining, you haven't seen daylight since you arrived, as unnoticed by Andy you worked right the way through dinner break to catch up and work through the huge pile of real paperwork on your desk as opposed to your strategically placed diversions.

So, the weather is a disappointment, but it doesn't come as a shock. It has been a wet and rainy day outside and for you inside since you woke up. You hate the rain and, in the hurry, to get things sorted this morning you forgot to put on an over coat. Rain drips onto the shoulders of your suit as you walk to the far end of the business park to get into your car. Within seconds you can begin to feel the wet soaking through the fabric making that white shirt of yours damp again, only this time it is the cold damp fluid produced by Mother Nature rather than your own body.

You start to walk a little faster, but with the extra pace you begin to focus more on what's ahead rather than what's below. Splash! A puddle jumps right up your trouser leg and grabs your sock, leaving it soaked, then to add insult to injury on its way down it seeps into the inside of your brogues.

"For fucks sake" you say out loud, stopping for a moment to rock your foot in your shoes, just to hear the soggy squelch echo back as if to prove to you they are wet! You look to the heavens and close your eyes to try and regain your composure.

The car seems so far away and all you really want to do is get home and go back to bed, hideaway and begin again tomorrow. This day really has been one that you'd prefer to move on from.

You start a little jog, desperate now to just reach the car and the sanctuary of dryness. Water splashes up your trouser leg as more floods your shoes, you don't even notice the puddles now, you just have to get into the dry. You run and run, hell bent on getting to your destination, ploughing through the streams of flood water that flow across your path like snakes.

You reach the little exit road from the car park you are crossing, the one that separates you from your car and as you pause to look both ways before crossing, a huge 4x4 hurtles past and straight through a puddle that has accumulated over a drain cover that has quite simply had enough rain and is refusing to accept any more, just like you.

You are now soaked from top to bottom and as you use the back of your hand to wipe the rain water from your face, you feel little pieces of gravel run down your cheeks which scratch your delicate skin. Once again you feel a million miles away from being clean and fresh like you did after the shower this morning. Quite ironic really when both events consisted of water running down your face. You try to let out a little chuckle at that, but your spirit is broken, you are defeated, you don't even have the will to do that.

You freeze for a moment, wanting to give the driver of the 4x4 a piece of your mind, but he is gone, disappeared into a spray of backwash as he heads home to a family that loves him and a happy home. Deep down you know he has no knowledge of what has just happened, which makes you even more angry.

You stamp your feet into the puddle that has just violated you and you cast your face up towards the sky again. Rain drops splatter on your cheeks, maybe they could wash away any gravel that you have missed, and you simply close your eyes and stand still, composure well and truly washed away.

Your temples are pulsing with anger and frustration. You can feel your blood pumping faster through your veins as you try and control your temper. Now is not a good time to lose it, neither is here a good place.

You stomp across the road without even looking to see if any traffic is approaching, maybe you are hoping there is, then they could help you end this hideous day, but lady luck is on your side for once and the road is clear. Or maybe she isn't and you have missed an opportunity to put you out of your misery.

You reach your car and fumble for the remote key from your trouser pocket. You find it and as you pull it out into the wet world, it slips through your fingers and into a small puddle next to your driver's door.

You let out a loud sigh and take a deep breath before bending down and retrieving it. Wiping the plastic casing off your already ruined suit jacket you press the button to unlock the doors. Nothing. You press again, this time using a little more force but still nothing.

"Come on!!!" you yell, not knowing if the malfunction is down to damaged caused by being dropped or by the fact it has been dropped in water.

"For fucks sake come on!" You press the remote even harder, pushing the little button concealed behind the plastic with your finger nail, leaving a little indentation where your nail has been. Still nothing.

"Arrrgh!!" you scream and punch the tiny little device over and over again, each time getting more animated and each time getting more furious.

"Beep, beep" the side lights of your car eventually flash, and you can get in. You snatch at the door handle and open it by almost riving the door off its hinges. You throw your brief case inside first, another little piece of temper dealt with and as it ricochets off the passenger window and onto the floor you can't help but feel a little tinge of satisfaction.

Next is your suit jacket, resisting the temptation to ring it out, you yank at the sleeves and hurl it with them still turned inside out onto the back seat. It doesn't really matter though because as you finally sink into the driver's seat you realise just how wet the shirt that seems to have been doomed from the minute you put it on this morning actually is.

You can feel it sticking to your skin as you lean back and put on your seat belt. You can feel the fibers of the fabric resting on your flesh, cold and damp, just like the way your day has been. You put the key in the ignition and take a deep breath before starting the engine and finally setting off for home.

"Let's hope that dizzy old witch isn't on her way home" you chuckle to yourself remembering the journey in this morning, as you pull out of the works car park. Unaware that that is the first time you have laughed all day.

TWO LOVERS

The hurt that grows inside with neglect can be volatile, harmful and aggressive but sometimes it's the sheer pain of the dagger driving straight through your heart that causes the explosion, causes the outburst and thunderstorm that has been brewing for so long underneath. All of which brings you down to your knees, thus so begins the fall.

You have tried to ride that storm for many years now, but each time it passes, you feel like you have made it into the light, a new wave of unhappiness rolls in. In the place you are now, that storm will never pass. It is always there rattling at the door. Blowing through the rafters so hard sometimes you think the whole roof is going to come off leaving you completely exposed and vulnerable.

Inevitably it eventually does, you are wide open to the elements. Naked and run down, you are now so weak that you are there for the taking.

Why did she treat you like this? Why do you feel like you're only here to serve whilst she provides? She is the breadwinner and you are nothing. The foolish man who under estimated the nest of snakes he was entering into all those years ago. If only you'd looked deeper past the beautiful haze of sunshine that polluted your vision, maybe you would have seen the beast lurking.

Maybe if you paid more attention to the bull you wouldn't have found yourself in such a vulnerable position. Maybe then you would have seen everything on the horizon and seen the truth for what it was. Maybe then you would be able to see clearly now.

Black clouds, thunderstorms, hurricanes and lightening shattering the purple haze of happiness, the soft glow of contentment obliterated into a million pieces by one fork of the golden, deadly strike of nature, like a star dying in the brightest Supernova ever.

It was all there for you to see, in the far off distance, but the beginning of the demise was right in front of your eyes if only you had looked. If only you hadn't been distracted, if only you hadn't fallen head over heels in love.

She never really wanted you, not really. She maybe thought she did, but all she was really after was a toy to play with on her terms. Something to pick up and put down when she wanted. Something to fuck and fuck around with when she wanted. An accessory to everything else that was more important in her life.

You fell for it in a big way, in fact you might as well had Toys R Us printed across your forehead.

More and more anger. More and more decayed root that was planted firmly and a rot that was set in motion the moment she went to work for him.

This was supposed to be the job that made her, both career wise and emotionally. Her 'big break' that's what she called it. Something she had worked so hard for and waited so long for. With this job she could help provide more and better, she could ease worries and she'd be happy. Well, she certainly achieved that, she was happy alright, just not with you.

You don't really remember the exact moment when it all changed or when you began to notice things were decaying. There wasn't really one set cut off point or trigger that made you think "hang on." But the outcome was inevitable the moment she set eyes on him, right from the start and the first meeting at the interview.

He could have anything he wanted, anyone he wanted. In return he could give her everything, nothing was an issue. He could probably even give her the world if she asked. In fact, the truth was that she probably didn't even need to ask he would just give it her anyway. No reason why, other than he did because he could and, in doing so he shattered everything you possessed, including the world you knew and loved.

The working late started very soon after she started the job, so did spending the money she earned on new work clothes, business suits that you always found so sexy, but the bedroom fun stopped around the same time as the job took over. Then came the meetings and eventually the business trips away that progressed from overnight stays to three or four days. You still feel physically sick at the thought of him fucking her in some expensive hotel room in those very same business suits, the ones that attracted you so much too, whilst you were stuck at home all alone.

It was after one such trip away that you decided that you were going to confront your suspicions and face up to the demon that was eating you up inside. Consuming your heart and soul before taking all of you.

She always got a taxi back home from the train station, that's what she told you anyway.

"No need for you to come out into the cold baby, I'll just grab a cab and a takeaway?" she used to say.

You were gullible and agreed. Looking forward to her returning and having some food together instead of beans on toast standing at the kitchen bench, you would just nod and kiss her on the top of the head, naive and foolish.

However, this one day you decide to surprise her at the train station, maybe you could go out for something to eat instead. Your intention fixed on making her return special for you both.

You hide around by the newsagent stand as her train approaches, suddenly you feel anxious, a knot tightens in your stomach as the smell of diesel and trains breaking fill the old Victorian construction. You are hoping your hunch is wrong and that maybe you are just a little paranoid and insecure, you are hoping with all your heart you are wrong.

The train stops, as streams of passengers descend onto the grey concrete platform, eager to be away from their hosting vehicle, rushing about to whatever is next in their busy little lives, like a little colony of worker ants setting off to do their chores. Under instruction and with their orders they scurry off on their missions, no time for anybody else.

You stand still, just like your life is doing, hidden and still you stand and scour the platform for the woman you would die for. The woman you love with all your heart.

There she is, slowly making her way down the three stairs right at the back of the train, so far back it's the last carriage. You don't realise at the time but the fact it was the final steps on the final carriage is so ironic. That split second of her coming through the door, smiling and looking so happy was so beautiful but also the last time she is yours.

Her overnight bag is slung over her shoulder, in her right hand is the leather laptop bag that you bought her last Christmas after work had given her a new works computer, so she could work wherever she was.

Her overcoat is open, revealing her buttoned up grey business jacket, a white blouse reared its innocent self from between the collars, open to reveal a very small piece of chest, stopping just above the cleavage, open and on display. Just like them, they are

so brazen and not even trying to hide the obvious sexual connection.
Her left arm is stretched way back behind her, it looks almost uncomfortable until you see the reason why. There he is holding her by the hand and helping her down the stairs. He too looks happy, his black pinstriped suit jacket open, as is his crisp white Italian shirt. No tie, the hairs of his chest protruding in a shameless flaunt of testosterone. It is obvious for the world to see that this isn't boss and secretary, this is two lovers returning from a trip of passion and lust. Ignore the business suits and laptop bags, this has been a fuckfest of two very attractive and successful people, one of which you thought belonged to you.
You take a step backwards in pure shock, forgetting where you are and crashing into the magazine stand you had been using as your disguise. An old lady perusing the TV Times straightens the stand and tuts at you before switching her attention back to next week's viewing.
 The distraction of your loss of balance means you have lost your quarry and you move away almost in a daze from the old lady, the TV Times and the rows and rows of Readers Wives magazines. You scour the horizon like a spy in a World War Two film, looking for the enemy, a stakeout you never wanted to be on, a stakeout that will lead to a fall out. The fallout that will ruin your life forever.
There they are, over near Costa. She is giggling at something he has said as he orders two cappuccinos', then he leans down and kisses her on the head. You can see the devotion in her eyes. He has just kissed her in the exact place that you kissed her yesterday morning as the taxi picked her up from the home you shared. The exact place that you kiss her every day, your place, the place that you can feel both her skin and her hair, the place that you smell the soft fragrance of her face cream but also the stronger, fresher smell of her fruity shampoo. You know every smell of her, if you close your eyes now you can still smell those smells. He has just kissed her there.
You move at the same pace that they do. Loitering far enough back not to be seen or raise attention, but close enough to be able to see. They stroll across the station hand in hand, he takes the laptop bag you bought her, as she carries the coffees in a grey

cardboard type tray in the hand it has vacated. They continue across the busy walkway, oblivious to all the people around, only interested in themselves, walking, talking and giggling, stopping occasionally for a quick peck of affection. They are oblivious to the world around them, more importantly maybe, they are oblivious to you.

Outside they walk between the cars that sit in uniformed lines in the car park. You dodge behind them, like a comical detective off a Two Ronnie's sketch, your heart is pounding with both hurt and an excitement not to be seen, but deep down the only emotions you know are shattered, you are broken beyond repair.

Suddenly they stop, he puts the bag you bought down. Reaching into the inside of his suit jacket he pulls out a car key and presses the button that opens the door. A bleep bleep noise echoes around the parking lot, as the red rear lights of a silver Porsche wink in your direction, almost mocking you with that little mischievous twinkle.

They pull together more closely than they have already and start to kiss. Passionately, his hands move all over her, clutching at her buttocks and the back of her neck. Your pulse starts to raise with hatred and hurt, you can feel the fury buzzing all over your body, touching senses that you never really used or knew existed come to think of it. You close your eyes and tilt your head back and begin to shake it violently, desperately trying to erase the image from your head. This can't really be happening, you were going to surprise her and take her out for a meal tonight. That's why you came, that is why you are here, because you missed her so much. The silly little piece of jealousy that you had aimed at her boss was nothing more than that, silly jealousy. This couldn't be happening, you are made for each other.

You shake your head faster from side to side, your eyes still scrunched shut into tight balls, trying to squeeze reality away. You open your mouth to scream but you know you cannot let any noise come out, that would blow your cover, so you just squeeze your eyes shut even tighter.

When you finally open them, they are gone. Exhaust fumes still linger in the space where the Porsche was parked. You stand still in shock, just staring at the empty space where your love died.

All that remains are exhaust fumes and as they begin to dissolve into the air, so does the power and meaning of your entire life.

TAXI FOR ONE

The taxi pulls away slowly, leaving her with her bags on the road at the top of the drive. Over two hours have passed since you watched her leave the train station with him. You watch from the sitting room window as the cab disappears into the distance before she starts to navigate the stony track of your drive. She watches it leave, unaware that you are watching, then she straightens her jacket and wriggles her shoulders. Slowly turning, she picks up her bags. As she does you notice her pretty, white lacy blouse is now fastened right up to the top. Her hair looks ruffled but as if she has made a huge effort to try and tidy it.

The rain starts to fall now, in the form of a fine annoying drizzle. Black clouds fill the view, forming a dark ring around a very dark situation, it's as if the powers that be knew.

She takes a deep breath and looks nervous, something she may have done a million times before, but you never noticed it. You were usually in the house straightening the cushions or wiping down the benches before you poured her a deep ruby red glass of Cabernet Sauvignon, ready to hand it to her the moment she walked through the door as you welcomed her back home.

Normally you are so pleased to see her return, the messiah that you worship walking back into your life, but today you are broken. Completely and utterly broken, your heart in pieces, like a mirror that has been dropped from an upstairs window onto the durable concrete below. Everything you have ever wanted in your life was shattered like that glass in the train station car park. There could be no coming back from this.

She turns to face the house, unaware that you are watching her through the window still. Her cheeks look flushed, her make up fresh, her outfit so blatantly pristine it's as if she has just put it on, not just stepped off a train and, deep down you know that of course she has.

Her hands fidget inside her jacket for her house keys, just like he had at the car park only hers are trembling with nerves. You think about rushing to open the front door and helping her, but instead you stay where you are. Your buttocks cemented to the deep, low windowsill of the sitting room. Even if you wanted to stand up you couldn't, your legs are like jelly. Even if you wanted to go and greet her with open arms, you couldn't.

She approaches the little gate to the yard and with a soft little squeak as it opens, she enters, she has returned home and to her real life, her life with you. Striding as if she is a woman on a mission she steps across the yard, purposely and focused, she is desperate to just get inside and get the meeting and greeting over with. Maybe then she will feel normal.
You sit and watch. The door handle eventually turns, enabling you to feel a little burst of fresh damp air as the front door opens.
"Hey baby" she says entering the home you have built up together. She says that every time she comes home, but this time you can hear the deceit in her voice. The tone is fake, unnatural and forced. For that you have no forgiveness and for the first time in your life you begin to hate someone.
Shocked at the brutality of the emotion, you stagger onto your feet, you actually do hate her. A hate that hurts more than any pain you have ever felt before. More painful than when your parents split up and more painful than when you were kicked unconscious down that back alley. Excruciating, agonizing sharp daggers cut into your chest and head, you feel as if your whole body is going to explode, the hurt and pressure is just too much.
"I saw you." You respond. Not letting her get her foot off the front door mat.
"I saw you at the railway station with him."
You can feel her stop still her tracks, her body in total shock at what you have just said. Everything stops. The creak of the front door, the ticking of the old clock on the mantel piece, everything stops. Tick tock, the pendulum swings and for a moment time stands still. Everything stands still. Your heart is beating fast in your chest, you can hear it above the ticking of the clock, your ears ringing with psychedelic bells, thundering away drowning out any other thoughts like a plague of locusts devouring everything in their path.
You wait, rigid, fixated and concentrating on the empty air, urging a response. Silence and nothing, all the years together and all the plans you made and when it comes down to it, when it really matters, she has nothing to say. No denial, no explanation, no breaking down in tears and a story of how it was all a mistake. All you hear is the soft click of the front door closing and her footsteps setting off back across the yard, seconds later you hear

her on her mobile calling a taxi and sobbing gently. You look back out of the sitting room window and just watch her standing there in the rain. Standing crying, but never looking back at the house or you. You want to go out and comfort her, tell her everything will be ok, that you can work it all out. However, your feet won't move even when you try. You are frozen with shock, numb with the pain, you physically cannot move.

Ten minutes later, the black cab takes her away in one big U turn. Sweeping past everything that you have shared, sweeping past the house, the views, the sheep, the fields, passing it all as you look on. For a split second you feel like you aren't the only one watching but you know there is nobody else, just your eyes playing tricks on you.

In the field furthest away stands the bull, upright and stern he stares, he has seen and heard it all. His head turns and follows the cab drive away down the lane, eyes tracking it until it moves out of sight.

You and him never saw her at home or as yours again.

LOSING IT

So, it can't all have been so bad can it? Surely it wasn't all as hurtful and vindictive as this? There were so many good times that must have been so valuable and outweighed the hurt and deceit you are left with now? Truth is you don't really know, you don't know what's true and what's lies anymore, fact or fiction. What was affection and what was manipulation. You are hurting so much that you no longer have any idea about anything anymore. Losing her has resulted in you losing yourself, you may as well of died that afternoon in the rain.
She never came back, she never got in touch and she never asked for anything from the home. She simply disappeared along with everything you had. A friend of yours once told you in your teens to enjoy the good times you were having with a new older, more experienced girlfriend you had recently become obsessed with. Five years your senior and an aerobics teacher, who wouldn't have.
"It never lasts" he stated over a Chinese takeaway one Friday night when you didn't have the money to afford a night on the town.
"Weeks down the line it will be shit like everything else and you'll get sick of her like all the others. Happens every time pal." You wish, as you tucked into a curry in total dismay at his comment, you'd thought about what he'd said. You wouldn't feel as hurt and as bitter as you did the day she walked away.
More than twenty years later he had been proved right, only it was she that had gotten sick of you. Still, it was shit, that part he had been one hundred percent correct. He'd have a good laugh at your expense now if he knew. Thankfully you were no longer in touch.
The girlfriend didn't last much longer than the curry that night, and thus your first step on this hazardous path of the opposite sex and obstacles between you and complete happiness began. Can you really trust anyone? Even when you think you have found your perfect soul mate, the one you were destined to be with. Can you fully trust them? You have asked yourself that question a million times since that day and every time your answer is the same. How can you know what is going on inside their head and perhaps even more importantly, how can you know the reasons for the actions and words they take? Do they

really love you or is it all a game? Did she really love you? What the fuck is love anyway?

All of these thoughts ran through your brain in the immediate days that followed that Sunday afternoon. As the days passed the pain didn't subside as you thought and hoped it would, instead it grew and grew, changing and developing, morphing itself into hatred and a feeling of complete and utter neglect. You gave her everything and she left you with nothing.

When the summer finally came, you cut the grass, making those little pathways through the tall stems of wild flowers and grass that she used to love. You stopped for a beer break like you always did, only this time you had to go to the fridge yourself to get it, no beautiful waitress service, then you sat and drank on your own in silence. You weeded the flower beds that she had created and spent endless nights alone in front of the wood burning stove that you bought together from the garden centre down the road that certainly knows how to charge a top price. You spent that Saturday afternoon together and having fun, you wanted the stove, she wanted the willow tree. You bought both, and whilst you spend the entire summer drinking beyond excess in solitude, you still can't look at the willow tree that you planted in the middle of the little garden hidden from view, your special tree in your secret garden.

That's what she used to call it, hidden right around the back of the house so you could only find it if you knew it was there, the day she left she might as well have boarded it up. You could never look on it in that way again, it was more like tending to the grave of a long lost relative. One that you only knew as a very small child so whilst you know who they were, your memories are completely fuzzy and full of nostalgia.

They say time heals, but you never found it that way. In fact, life begins to hurt more and more the quicker that it moves on. Every day the pain grows and grows, every day the wound seems to break down further, the gap between the edges of flesh getting wider and wider. Every day you lose yourself deeper into the darkness and depths of misery and decay. Somebody should have just shot you that day she left, like they do an old horse. It would have been fairer and easier for you in the long term.

Walking around the house that had been 'your' home and the gardens you had established together, your heart aches more and more. You have tried to repair it and move on, but the opposite has happened, the flesh around the wound has now died and with that the healing process stops. The tissue is now fighting against itself, decay and death begins to consume the flesh around it. Inside you are dying and mentally you are unable to do anything to prevent it.

You try to carry on as if nothing has happened, putting on a brave face to everyone around you, but deep down you are crumbling and losing control, breaking apart. You are beginning to slip; thus, the bull is coming more and more into your dreams. Invading your conscience and intuition like Hitler's army marching across Europe, the bull is taking everything. Sweeping in and giving no regard to anything positive that has been there prior to the decaying path he leaves behind him.

Work loses your interest, your friends lose your interest, football loses your interest, life in general becomes mundane and unbearable. So much so that you lose all interest in that too.

You begin to revert back into yourself, refusing invitations to go out by always having an excuse not to attend, but perhaps even sadder was the fact that you never have any intention of accepting an invite in the first place.

When you do have to go out you begin to struggle. Crowds are everywhere, traffic lights become a major issue, as do pelican crossings. You avoid busy places, preferring to do your shopping on line than going to the supermarket. Everybody is out to get you it feels, everybody is watching, everybody wants to bring you down, not just the bull.

You are on your own and have no comeback. You don't have the drive or desire to rebel or fight back. You are a loser who has reached this miserable and difficult stage of your life by making bad choices and decisions. Your entire existence has amounted to nothing. Your being has been a complete waste of time and now after all of these years you have nothing left to show for it.

You are alone and beginning to slip further, of that there is no doubt and the bull is watching and loving every minute of it. He is there to push you down if needed, but you are doing a good job of self-destruction yourself. All he has to do now is stand back and wait, wait and watch.

A friend told you about six months after that Sunday that she had been dumped by the boss, social media had been the source of his information, so it must have been true! She'd caught him cheating with the new office junior. She was only eighteen and had great perky tits he said, your ex had taken it badly, moved out of the big detached house on the golf course and was seeking counseling.

You felt no sympathy, although a little bit of pride flooded back due to the fact that, despite what she had done and what they had put you through, you hadn't crumbled and sought medical advice. Even that was false pride though, because deep down you knew that maybe you should have. Maybe that could have saved you.

Instead you sit every night alone and drink. You begin sleeping on the sofa in front of the fire because it is warm, especially as she is no longer there to hold and cuddle you, to share her body heat or for her to share yours. You get more and more lonely with every turn of the page on your calendar, more and more desperate.

Every night you drink until morning comes and then watch the sun rise. Beautiful reds, yellows and purples as the sun beckons in a new day. You understand none of this though, it is simply another day in your long life sentence, another day that you somehow have to survive. Each beautiful sunrise you hope will be your last and the beginning of the day that finally sees you put out of your misery.

As you lie and watch the beginning of every new day, you feel nothing. No excitement, no anticipation, just emptiness.

You never feel refreshed or rested, you are never ready to jump up off the sofa ready to make a fresh start, sometimes you don't even know if you have had the privilege have slept or not.

INSOMNIA

The rain beats down against the window of the big chain coffee shop, blurring your view and distorting your vision of the outside world and life itself. Steamy windows overlooking a grey and even less appealing existence, the angry skies look to be about to get darker as heavier and more hostile clouds creep menacingly over the roof of the bus station, setting off towards the shopping centre. Heading directly and almost intentionally towards you, you can almost see the hatred in the storm approaching, it is coming for you, solely you.

A guy from behind the counter heads to your direction, you say guy because you're not really sure if he's a qualified barista or just a table wiper, anyway he is bringing you caffeine and that is the most important thing in the world right now.

Kevin leans and places your double espresso down on the worktop type bench you have chosen to sit on this wet morning, a bench that faces the outside world, so you can keep an eye on the horrors that lurk there. You can monitor the storm and see just how much time you have to avoid a soaking when you dash back to the car.

You didn't sleep very well again last night, your brain just never quite shut down enough to allow the z's to flow. Shut down, what a strange term to use when the rest of your body is running on well below empty. Surely your brain should be fighting to keep you alive?

You thank Kevin, you know this is what he goes by as that is what it says on his name badge along with a coffee bean logo. His skinny frame hardly fills the polo shirt he is instructed to wear, the hoops just make him look flat rather than wide, whilst his drainpipe legs are far too long for the very straight fit work pants he has somehow managed to squeeze into. Not the image he was planning to portray on his graduation, still thanks to the government this was just a temporary means to an end until he paid off his student loan. Then he'd be able to concentrate on the career he'd studied for, which of course was?

You look him straight in the eyes, hoping direct eye contact would help you suck out the information you were looking for, tell you what this young and ill looking future hope of the country was planning to do with this life he was just beginning. You stare more intensely, surely you'll be able to extract a clue,

but not a thing from Kevin. He doesn't even notice you looking, his brain is stuck in the rut of his days work. The mundane sucking the very zest for life out of him, until his shift is finished. At least he has that to look forward too.
You nod in his direction to emphasise your gratification as he leans past you to collect a half eaten muffin on a plate next to you, that has obviously been left behind by the last world watcher.
Again nothing, Kevin must really love his job, that's clear by his natural customer care skills and typical of society today. Ignorance and self importance gone mad, they can't even return a head nod.
"Made for the job!" you mutter under your breath, having finally lost interest in the specimen before you and have a little chuckle to yourself. You reposition yourself on your tall bar stool and move your jacket and bag further along the bench now the cake has gone.
You look down at the few crumbs that Kevin didn't think required to be moved and it sets your brain off again analyzing something so simple, yet other people wouldn't have even noticed it, so much so that you have a quick look around in case the rest of the customers can hear the whirring sound of the cogs inside your weary brain turning over.
Who owned the plates Kevin has just removed and why did they leave the muffin half eaten? Were they disturbed? Or did they simply not like it? Maybe a loved one came and waived from outside and they were so excited they simply put the muffin down, pulled up the hood on their jacket to beat the rain and rushed out to meet them. The huge embrace and kiss taking away the cold, wet imposing factor of the rain. Did they turn and walk away with their arms around each other? Totally engrossed in spending the day together. The muffin long forgotten as they giggle and joke on their way out of sight.
Just like you and her used too.
Maybe the bus just turned up a little early and the eater had to quickly gather all of their papers and bags, not having time to put on their jacket and instead they threw it over their sleeve and completely forgot about the sweet breakfast they were enjoying just seconds earlier. Splashing through the puddles they just made

it in time, jumping on the bus just as it was about to pull away much to the driver's disgust.
Or maybe the clouds came earlier than originally expected and lured the owner of the muffin outside before sweeping them away never to be seen again. Forever living in the grey and wet. Forever living alone and in the eye of the storm.
It won't take you though, you're sure of that and as you rub your eyes and pinch the top of your nose where it joins your eye sockets, you softly shake your head in realisation of where you are. You will never know the story of the muffin and in all honestly it doesn't really matter.
"It's just a fucking muffin!" you say under your breath
"Just a half eaten muffin!" You close your eyes for a second as if you wish that when you open them the evidence of the crumbs and the muffin will be gone, erasing it from your mind as if it has never been there.
When you open them, you focus on the hot steam rising from your espresso and take a deep sniff of the caffeine overload sitting there in the tiny coffee mug.
You pick it up and bring it up to your lips, struggling to get your fingers through the tiny little handle. It's as if at that moment you've become a giant at a teddy bears picnic and as the miniature mug hits your mouth you open up and throw the dark, murky liquid down your throat in a oner. Ignoring the fact that it is so hot, ignoring the fact it is so strong and ignoring the fact that you'd be better off with something healthier and containing more vitamins. You need something right now to get you up and on with the day. Like a junkie needing to score, you need that caffeine rush to give you that kick start and an adrenalin boost. You need the beans to clear the mist, the mist from not having any sleep.
You slept, for want of a better word, on the couch again last night. Maybe it would be more accurate to say you lay on the sofa, you certainly cannot recall any sleep. The wood burner was on and there seemed no point in venturing into the cold and lonely bedroom that you used to share with her. Going through to what used to be your paradise once you'd finished working on the paperwork that you had brought home from work in order to catch up, after spending another day in a fuzzy mental haze.

What was the point of going through there and climbing into an empty bed? What was the point of anything?
Plus, you'd poured yourself a large whiskey and were relaxing as the logs crackled away. Surely this would help you sleep? Or so that is what you thought.
That's what you told yourself anyway, but very quickly it became apparent that that wasn't the case. Even a second whiskey that was more like a half pint didn't do the trick.
You lay on the sofa almost corpse like, not tossing and turning, not crunched up snoring in the fetal position, you just lay there like a snapshot from the morgue, stretched out on your back with your arms folded across your chest, it was as if you had died. Maybe inside you had?
The moon sent streaks of pure and unpolluted light through the undressed windows and across the ceiling as you lay there and stared, stared at nothing and thought about absolutely nothing.
Twice you got up and went to the toilet, four times you passed the bedroom door, twice going and twice returning, not once did the invite of the comfortable bed that you shared so many nights with her make its way into your brain. Zombie like you trudged back down the hall and back onto the couch.
Three times you got up and put more wood into the log burner. Feed the beast, feed the beast, feed the beast.
Morning came around and the chores started. Into the kitchen, still wearing the shorts and the Star Wars tee that you had been 'relaxing' in last night, you squint as a car's full beam of headlights whips around the kitchen as a farm worker passes your home on the way to work. You didn't close any of the curtains last night. Why would you? What's the point? Nobody ever passes this way and even now that somebody had it didn't bother you that they could have looked in. Nobody is interested in you, why would they even bother to look.
Most important jobs first, cupboard for a mug, any mug, and then straight to the percolator that has been keeping your coffee warm since 6am. That was when you pressed snooze on the alarm for the very first time hoping you may even get a quick ten minutes sleep. Wishful thinking.
The espresso has given you a little buzz but not enough. You need more if you are to get through the long and miserable day

ahead. Leaving your possessions on the bench you stand and turn towards the counter. Looking for a familiar face you see Kevin has actually got his coat on and is heading towards the door with a packet of Benson and Hedges in his hand. His addiction comes before your addiction it seems.

"How can I help?" asks a fresh faced ginger haired girl as your gaze shifts from the back of Kevin's hoodie and you turn back towards the back drop of huffing and puffing silver coffee machines.

You glance down to look to see her name badge, then realise it's in a very awkward position on her breast. Raising your head again you see her pale and freckly cheeks have flushed with blood in embarrassment.

"Erm double espresso please Lianne" you glance at the badge again just to emphasise the point and explain why you were looking at this young girl's chest.

"Double Espresso, please."

Lianne makes your latest hit and pushes it towards you on a brown plastic tray, face still reflecting the misfortune of your gaze. You pay your £2.20 and ignore the tray, lifting the minute cup and saucer and scurrying back to your seat in the window. Embarrassed, awkward and completely self aware, every customer in the shop has just watched you ogle at the breasts of a girl young enough to be your daughter. What if she thinks you were actually looking at her breasts? You would be seen as a pervert, a sex pest, everyone would hate you even more. You look hurriedly all around just waiting for security to come and remove the dirty old man from the shop window.

Of course, all you see is a crowded coffee shop full of people going about their own business, nobody is looking for or at you and Lianne is now too busy serving a line of customers to think of anything sexual whatsoever. You shake your head as if to get rid of the illusion and turn back to stare outside, back to the depressing world of reality.

The clouds are still coming and gathering in numbers as more line up behind the biggest, blackest sack of rain you have ever seen. They are still heading in your direction, coming for you. You start to recognize shapes within the clouds, simple everyday objects whose guise has been taken by the white waters above.

One looks like a car of the Mr Men cartoon, one looks like a butterfly that has just landed, its wings all spread out to declare its beauty. Only this butterfly has no colour but whites and grays. Then comes the biggest, darkest cloud. Full to the brim of water and anger, so volatile it looks like it could explode into a heavy down pour at any moment. The droplets that form the cloud are twisting and turning inside, all jostling for space and pushing another out of line to get to the front. None of them step out of the shape though, none of them venture outside the lines, the bulls head stays perfectly in tacked.

When did you last sleep properly? Days? Weeks? Months? You can't really remember. It feels as if you have not slept since the day she left you and walked away from everything, but surely there will have been nights you got your head down for even a few hours, rested your eyes just a little. It doesn't feel that way though, it feels like you have never slept at all, ever.

There was that one time though that you managed it, on the train when you were heading to London for those series of meetings. Whether it was the motion of the train, or the fact that your body had been so relaxed at actually not doing anything as you plundered your way across Blighty's countryside of fields, rivers and council estates, you seemed to be able to sleep quite easily. A series of power naps until you fell into the land of sleep and dreams, deep sleep that seemed almost alien to you. Yes, there were the dreams and the rocking from left to right as the train weaved along the track, but you felt rested. At least you did until the dream where the bull came. A huge black figure that loomed over you as you made your way through a flowery meadow in the sunshine. You were happy until he came, that much you can remember from the dream. Happy and alive.

In fact, come to think of it the bull always seems to come to you when you are weak enough to fall asleep. No matter where you are, on a train or on the bus, on the couch or when you pulled the car over into a layby as your body gave in to the long blink, you always seem to have the same dream. There is always that huge bull. Staring right back at you with fierce amber eyes and steam pulsating from his nostrils.

You pinch the bridge of your nose again, and softly shake your head to regain your composure. Staring out of the window you see it is still raining, the clouds are still coming, with the world's people are still rushing around like worker ants. All of them on a mission, all of them busy and serving a purpose in a bigger web of meaning, whilst you sit alone on the outside watching and gazing in. Or are you on the inside looking out? Either way your existence goes unnoticed, you are insignificant, in this bleak and glum portrait you are nothing worth framing.

Tired and run down you watch people going about their daily chores and wish that you had the same motivation and drive. It never occurs to you for a second that they may have not slept last night either. Maybe the bull comes to them too.

The second espresso smells as good as the first, but this time you are determined to gather at least a little enjoyment from it. You take a small sip, again being very careful when handling the undersized porcelain. The earthy taste fills your mouth leaving your tongue dry but wanting more. You take another sip and savor every drop as it leaves a heavy trail of caffeine as it passes through your body. Soaring through your veins like a drug from a needle, you finally have your hit. The junkie has scored.

How times have changed, how you have changed. Your memory jumps back to a time when you were a kid and thought it was a grown up thing to do to pinch a sip of your father's black coffee whilst he wasn't looking. Other kids maybe did it with their parent's cigarettes, for you it was the power and scent of that little bean.

You did of course find it vile and questioned how he could drink and enjoy it. In fact, you questioned how he could even drink it, never mind enjoy it!

Deep, thick and tar like is how you remember that first ever sip. Yet here you are many years later sitting in a huge chain of shops drinking the deepest, richest, strongest caffeine product on their menu and doing so because of a need rather than for pleasure, serving your addiction.

Drinking it because you need it. Drinking it because it's all you have to help you stay alive.

BEELZEBUB

The bull comes to you every night as you try to sleep. Although the term 'sleep' is in itself a questionable use of the word. Your life has become a walking nightmare where the comfort of sleep has become nothing more than a dream that seems impossible to achieve.

Every single night whilst your lights are switched off he arrives at your house, circling the building till he finds your bedroom, circling the house exhaling bellows of grey steam from his huge, wide open nostrils. Circling until he finds you. A predator moving in on a kill.

A huge monster of an animal, with horns that would fill an entire fire place if he was ever caught and sacrificed in the barbaric manner of yesteryear. This bull dwarf's any creature you have ever been close to, even though you aren't fully aware that he is there. Even the animals you have seen on television are nothing compared to him. This being is so big he blots out everything that has been, everything to come and everything in the immediate world, including the moon and the stars. Bringing darkness and blackness, your stalker blocks out eternity, for eternity.

Black as the night that brings him on his journey to you and as deep and dark as everything sinister that creeps around after the sun has gone down he watches you, only you, you are his quarry. You are all he wants. His mission to come and find you is not a good sign, nor one you would welcome if you were aware of it, but your ignorance to his existence makes you even more vulnerable. In fact, his mission for you can only lead to one thing, decay, a deep descent that seems inevitable.

The moon glistens in the sky behind him and slithers of the white light reflect off a huge silver ring that penetrates the nostrils of this gigantic beast as he stands stock still and stares through your bedroom window.

Glowing like a diamond but with the danger of a drawn sword, you are the subject of his interest. The victim and easy prey. The remoteness of your cottage retreat is working against you, isolation means everything is black, no street lights to display his huge frame, all there is to make out in the blackness is the ring, his piercing amber eyes and that intoxicating grey mist of the breath he blows towards you, oxygen from which he has taken everything he wants and then spat out. Just as he will you.

Since the day you were born he has been following your story, but for months now he has been standing outside and looking in, watching you, assessing you, weighing you up. Waiting for the right time to venture inside and take you down that bitter and twisted road that only goes in one direction. He will lead you to your final destination, forcing you if you try and resist as you slip down the endless slope to oblivion where you will rest forever, alone.
Regardless of the weather he is there and no matter whether it be rain, fog or snow the bull comes with the moonlight. A weathered and experienced hunter, nothing will distract him from the trail of his prey. He has been sent to find you and to watch you, to hunt you and take you down. Which is exactly what he will do.
Like all alpha males though, firstly he has to figure out what it is he's up against and prepare himself for every eventuality. He will not fail, he never does. There will be no rest until he has completed his mission and you are gone.
Fire rages in his eyes as he stares, never taking his gaze off you as you toss and turn in your very slender and delicate sleep. It is almost as if you know you are being watched. Asleep but awake, still but unrested, unconscious but subconscious, the nightmares intensified around the time the bull turned up.
Little puffs of condensation form on your window pain and then disappear just as quickly as he breaths slowly in and out, fresh and clean that becomes evil and darkness exhaling onto the clear purity of the glass. In the dark his breath is almost tangible as it spouts from his huge flared nostrils. In and out, in and out, his breath keeping in time with your beating heart, mimicking you and mocking your life force as something that is nothing more than mediocre entertainment.
Every night he is there and every night he watches, getting closer to the window every time. He wants to come in, he wants to sniff you and work out exactly what you are. Maybe more to the point, who you are and why he has been sent, but he knows he has to be patient and wait for his moment.
The year seems to move on faster than the world that engulfs you on a daily basis and as December approaches the bull becomes even bigger and even more inquisitive, even more determined to complete his mission. Even more determined to get inside. It is as

if he is becoming bigger, more powerful the more you slip. He is feeding off your loneliness, fear and anxieties. He is sucking life from within you and using it to feed himself and make him more powerful and unbeatable. By the time you face him you will be so weak and he will be so strong, using you like a steroid to gain advantage. You will never be able to defeat him.

It is on the 23rd of December, just two days before Christmas, when he finally decides you are low enough for him to venture into your home for the first time and stand over you as you lie motionless in your bed.

The dogs are sleeping and do not stir, you are sleeping and also do not stir as the stench of impurity and purgatory fills the room, such a strong smell that even in your lumbered state your nostrils waken to its appearance. You have never smelt anything like it before but in some way the sickening and putrid odor smells both familiar and unrecognisable. Dark and suffocating, the smell of death coming to collect.

His sheer mass fills the room, leaving nowhere to run or to hide. His aura fills the whole house and undoubtedly there is a sense of an evil presence behind all of this.

Standing over you he blows hot steam out his nostrils just inches from your face, you scrunch your face up as if a fly has landed on your nose, and mutter something under your breath that goes something like:

"Get off, shoo, I'm trying to sleep." But for once you are asleep, fast asleep, dead to the world, literally.

The bull doesn't get off, nor does he 'shoo.' In fact, your petulant dismissal does nothing but serve to annoy him and instead he moves even closer.

His eyes now glowing red like an ember from a flame, the amber gone and replaced by a more furious crimson glow. Snorting as he moves he sniffs you from head to toe and as he moves his enormous head back up from the base of your bed he licks the sheets as if to taste you, before continuing on up your neck, chin and face.

The bull has the taste of you now, he has gathered your scent and will continue to come and watch you until the day he finally is given the order to come and take you to his master. He is patient and knows the time will come soon, and when it does he will be

ready to take you on that grave descent to the fires. You are getting lower and lower, your spirit is broken but also your mental state is sliding beyond any conceivable normality.
That day is getting closer and closer.

LONELINESS

The National Park stretches into a desolate oblivion. A dank and barren place with a small sign pushed deep into the undergrowth to mark its beginning, but from where you are standing now it looks as if there can be no end, this is the very edge of the world, miles and miles ahead, it is the edge of your world at least. The mist hovers just above the grass, the dew glinting on each and every blade in early fingers of daylight. A new day creeping out from behind the blackness of night, like a sea retreating to shores new, leaving behind in its wake a cluster of rock pools all of which contain tiny bursts of life which have been hidden away under the deep and dark water.
There is no wind, everything is still. One drop of crystal like liquid appears as if it is about to drop from one blade of grass that is just a little taller than all the others, innocence and purity untouched, but nothing else moves. You are in a place time forgot, time and everyone else. Nobody else would want to be here at this time of day, when nothing else happens, but in an ironic twist you cannot help but think that is their loss. There is nobody else here to see such purity, you are alone. All alone.
Heather glows in the aura of a fresh start. Deep plums, pinks and purples provide a tangled carpet under the grey hiking boots on your feet, contrasting nicely with the earthy hue of the stems and storks. Deeper down still you can see the prehistoric root formation set out like a deadly trap for some unsuspecting rambler to come unstuck. Not you though, you move forward carefully, making sure your feet don't get caught in the gnarly undergrowth. It's a long and testing journey that you've set off on, but one you feel you have to do. Maybe, just maybe it will all be worth it if you can make it to the summit, more than just a walk, you will have achieved something for the first time in a long time.
Once upon a time you were aiming to go right to the top of the hill that stands in front of you now, man conquering nature. Something off the bucket list, that's how you saw it, but now the journey has started you have no option to climb. You have to make the climb, no turning back, there is only you here to keep yourself on the move, only yourself to rely on and only yourself to keep yourself safe. You are alone.

Setting off, you are quietly content. Despite the loneliness, you are in a beautiful place with fantastic views, almost panoramic. Surrounded by god's wonder in nature and wildlife, you certainly aren't fazed by having no human company. You are used to it now anyway, in fact the solitude gives you a little tingle, it makes you notice more around you and take it all in.

This beautiful place has been on your doorstep for years, at last you are doing it. Determined you block out the solitude and search for positives. Early morning song birds fill your head with a little cheery buzz, although the mist blocks the composer from your vision, you take a little comfort from knowing that you are not completely alone. There is life out here after all. For all you know they could be some kind of wild man eating air born creatures, but for now you are quite happy that the larks bringing you this morning song are ones that mean you no harm, a feathered friend and companion by song to keep you company on your climb to the sky.

You take your first steps onto the carpet of green and purple, and head north, setting off towards the peak that looms so far away in the distance. Closing behind you the gate to the footpath, you are closing behind you the gate to civilization. Closing behind you the gate to the rest of the world, but the truth is you don't really care. Civilization closed the gate on you a long, long time ago.

Your grey hiking boots move forward, left right, left right gliding through the sopping grass, the shade of your footwear getting darker as the morning dew soaks into the fabric, leaving a tide line around the toes just below where the laces start. You too are leaving a mark as your footsteps leave a flattened trail through the glazed stems.

Suddenly you stop, your right foot hovering inches above the grass, something moved and has caught your eye. Thankfully your senses and body are still quite alert and fresh despite it being so early, you let out a little sigh of relief as realise you haven't taken the life of the creature that was minding its own business below. Eager to get somewhere and eager to do something. You slowly bend to your honkers to get a closer look, your knees giving out a little click as you bend. You move a clump of grass to one side and reveal a slug that is making its way to wherever a slug goes to during the daytime. In no way in a hurry and leaving behind a slimy trail showing where it has been, so sparkly and fine that you could follow it all the way back through the undergrowth and find out exactly where a slug goes in the night if you wanted too.

Busy, busy little life, your own life suddenly feels so small and insignificant. Such different species, but so similar, like this slug you are battling against the landscape just to get where you need to go. You take a moment to lean closer, eager to see more. Amazed by the beautiful colours in the slug's camouflage, all you had ever thought of before was brown and slime, creepy and greasy, but up close it looks as if it has been specially sent there by the government with brown, tan and green patches all over its sleek, smooth skin, some kind of special force sent to conquer the gardens, hills and everything plant like in Britain.

You watch it move, wondering how it manages to glide over such terrain with no legs when you find it so difficult with two! Every obstacle seems massive to this little guy, yet it pushes itself along with ease, combating every hindrance in its way with sheer determination and such elegance. Its movements are stealth like, passing over blade after blade of grass which such ease and without alerting anything or anyone. Anyone but you that is. Was it fate or coincidence that you both happened to be at the same blade of grass at the exact same time? Especially when there are miles and miles of grass stems out here?

You stoop a little further forward, looking closely at the creature's optical tentacles, wondering what it is that it sees? Surrounded by such beautiful countryside but does he really see the view? You wonder if the slug sees the grass as green? Is the heather purple? Or can it even see the flowers at all given the big difference in size. Can it see where it's going? Or does it see where it has been? Does it know you are there? Can it see you? The thought suddenly makes you jump back a little. You know that you are alone from any human contact out here, but you never once stopped to think that the animals that undoubtedly surround you could actually be watching you, taking in your every movement, always on their guard and ready to run away or directly at you!

You stand up with a start, your whole body suddenly uncoiling like a spring. Tenaciously you lift your feet, right first then left, making sure you give this very silky hermaphrodite plenty of room. Over compensating actually, taking huge exaggerated steps, you look like a pantomime villain comically stalking his unsuspecting pray. He's behind you.

Setting off you head northwards and upwards, at this stage the plain stretches out in front of you, wide and open. No need for paths or tracks just yet, you have the run of natures carpet, this truly is the wonderful and limitless great outdoors.

You stride on, a few hundred yards further up you cross a little dip in the landscape, a tiny little valley that has been formed by the forces of nature over the years, deep and now there forever. On coming up the other side you see the true vastness that lies ahead. Turning back to face the way you've come your eyes scour the landscape, back down and over the dip, through the grass. You quickly skip the area where the slug somehow gave you the uncomfortable feeling of being watched and picture it there now staring back at you. Watching you and knowing you have nobody else close, vulnerable and easy prey, you are alone.

Past his watching gaze your eyes take you further afield. The gate you came through is just a dark spot on the green horizon. Your eyes pan around the scenery that is beautifully laid out before you. To the right there is nothing but fields and the odd cluster of trees, to the far left there is a splattering of small settlements, farms and hamlets, then further out into the distance you can see the soft haze of energy that surrounds the town. It is too far away for you to see anything, but you close your eyes and can imagine the hustle and bustle that is beginning to unravel as thousands of people begin to get up and begin their day.

Thousands of people, yet not so far away there is you. You and here, beautiful and lonely, something so great and something so small. The incredible mass that is this earth and the insignificance of you on your own.

Your eyes flick upwards and look at the horizon on which the town has cast a shadow. Even the clouds around there are different, not as pure and whilst the mist is obviously having a distorting effect on all you see, you know that down there is different. The air, the sound, the ambiance, it's all so different out there in the big wide world. You should know, your very existence down there on a day to day basis has ruined your life.

Turning to walk forward you again notice the magnitude of the task that you have set yourself and striding on your thoughts flicker to the last time you were here, just a week after your eighth birthday. You were so young and pure, an innocence you only realised was so special the older you became. Nothing more than a child, untainted by the pollution of life, if only you could go to the clock and turn back the hands of time.

Your parents brought you here. You, your sister and your best friend Pete. Your sister was six years older than you, and of course still is, but at those ages six years may well have been sixty. Whilst you were blown away by so much greenery, space and freedom, she was clearly missing her friends and all the things fourteen year old girls do.

Cheryl made sure that everyone on the trip knew just how much she despised being there, although at first it bothered you, you soon put her huff out of your mind. After all you were here for your birthday. Today was all about you.

Pete was like you, he loved the open space and was running around like a mad person desperately trying to cover every blade of grass that lay on this beautiful landscape. The freedom was all new to him, back home in the town he lived in one of the cluttered council streets, where people were everywhere. Everyone seemed to have more than 3 brothers or sisters, and quite often the grandparents lived next door or even shared the small abode with the rest of the family. Freedom and space were as alien to him as the Rain Forests or Sahara Desert.

He didn't really get a great deal of attention at home being the youngest, so being in the great outdoors and centre of attention with you meant the world to him. Dressed in his brother's hand me down Adidas tracksuit and running wild, this freedom was so new and to him this seemed just like heaven. A wilderness paradise that showed him there was more to life than kicking a football around black roads of tarmac filled with litter or playing knock nine doors.

To you both it was euphoric. Eight years old and feeling very mature, the whole world seemed to have been laid out in front of you and this afternoon indeed it did. You were so happy, so content. You noticed your sister's usual disapproval of the day's events, that all came with her age and her infatuation with boys, but you didn't notice the tension between your parents. In fact, you hadn't noticed the tension between them that happened on a daily basis. Why would you? You were a child and only eight years old.

Your father had been working a lot of hours lately. His company was trying to secure a big contract that would hopefully lead to a big pay rise and promotion. Funny how there is always the pull of promotion, the promised land around the next corner, but in your experience that carrot leads to nothing but the end. Same was true for your mother, that pay rise meant nothing if it resulted in a lack of attention to her and more importantly at the expense of much needed and much valued family time. All so precious.

The argument from after work on the Friday evening had rolled onto that Saturday morning, but you were too intent on enjoying your birthday day out to realise. How you wish you'd noticed the raised voices and slamming doors almost every day, that way you may have been a little bit more prepared.

To you and Pete it was the best day ever. You ran and slid down grassy slopes on your knees, marking your jeans with stains that never came out and at lunchtime you had the greatest picnic ever. Cheese sandwiches, pickled onion Space Raiders, Iced Gems, chocolate Dipsticks, all of your favorites. Perfect party food for the perfect party. Pete wasn't used to such special treats which lead to him devouring them all as if it was his last ever meal, but you weren't offended by his eating habits, you were happy he was having fun with you, enjoying your birthday. He was your best friend in the whole wide world and it felt great to be able to make him happy.

Cheryl picked at a bowl of salad whilst listening to Wet,Wet,Wet on her Walkman. Your parents sat drinking coffee, facing the opposite direction in utter silence. Neither of them even noticed the beautiful view they had all to themselves.

The afternoon was almost a carbon copy of the morning. Fun, running, playing and running, playing and then some more. Everything was just perfect for you and Pete, then you found a little stream. Your parents told you not to go too far away, but when the sun glistened off the fast flowing little brook, you both just sprinted off in that direction, horses drawn to water. You glanced back once, knowing deep down that you shouldn't be going so far from them, but that's when you saw them shouting at each other and waiving their hands in the air, how ironic that the fighting you had never noticed before had suddenly raised its ugly head and was staring you right in the face, today of all days. Both parents were totally oblivious to you looking, or even as to where you were. The fury that controlled the pair of them was blocking their vision, maybe their judgment but that is their concern and not yours. That day you had other things of importance, that day your mind was filled with things for you. Kids things and best friends.

A quick flick of your eyes to the left saw Cheryl lying flat on her back, knee's pointing to the air and her head bopping in time to some far away beat. You just know that it will have been Marti Pellow that was blocking her vision. In her world she'll be on stage with them right now, singing and dancing like she is Madonna, totally lost in a teenage dream that will of course lead nowhere. Girls her age were all the same, all wanted to be pop stars, all of them wanted rock star boyfriends, the harsh reality though was that the boyfriend never came along and none of them ever made it. It would be no different for your sister.

Pete had stolen a lead on you, he's wasn't very athletic but had still put you to shame, if you hurried that lead would not become irretrievable. You turned your back on your family and ran, another irony that set a precedent for the rest of your life. You ran as fast as you ever had, faster than all the clichés, faster than the wind, as if your life depended on it and within seconds you were level with Pete. Side by side you stride out together, happiness stretched across both your faces as your arms ran in sync with your legs like horses in the Grand National, only yours were now going that little bit faster.

You edged ahead and by the time the stream came you were in full flow, ahead by a furlong. Your speed had grown, meaning you were in full flight when the edge of the little ravine that borders the water came into your stride. Without thinking you lept, swooshing your arms up to help you gain height and distance, like an Olympic long jumper. Adrenaline alone took you into the air and over the stream. You landed in a bundle on the other side with a crash, but you didn't feel any pain, you were too busy laughing to be hurt. Laughing and shouting "Yes! Yes!"

as you lept back to your feet once more and started bouncing up and down. Adrenalin pumping fully through your body, perhaps for the first time in your entire life, the sweet taste of victory ran through your body.

Your jubilation was short lived though, as suddenly you heard a snap and a squeal just behind you. Pete! You turned but it was too late, your pal had never been as athletic as you and he had completely misjudged the ravine. Part of his tibia bone was protruding from his navy tracksuit bottoms, as he slumped head down into the water squealing in pain, with mud and blood splashed all over his face. You could see the break was bad, even from where you were standing.

The water continued to glisten but then it was all so sinister as the sun also caught the fresh white spear of bone that was protruding from his shin. Your parents finally stopped arguing and turned to look at where the noise was coming from, startled and almost unaware of where they were, the argument has taken such a hold of them both, then the penny dropped and they began to run towards you and Pete. Your sister didn't move. She was lying on her back, headphones on playing air drums, she was completely oblivious, you often wondered if she would have come even if Marti Pellow wasn't drowning out the screams and hysteria that was now taking place.

Pete's leg was shattered that day, He still walks with a little limp today. You know that because you bumped into him in the Tap and Spile just a few months ago. It was as if you were both strangers who had never really seen each other before, but somehow shared a dark secret. He acknowledged your good wishes but refused your offer of a pint. It was as if he had never forgotten or forgiven you for beating him in the race that day, for pushing him so hard that he ended up and disfiguring himself for the rest of his life. He blamed everything on you. Only you.

A week after that birthday incident your dad left the family home. You can count on one hand the number of times you have seen him since, certainly less than the figure of that last birthday all together, the last day you ever spent all together, the last day as a family.

A shadow darkens your face. You have almost forgotten where you are and just walked in zombie fashion as you continue your ascent. You look up towards the sky and notice that the mist is beginning to lift as little patches of blue sky begin to poke through the gloom. The shadow passes over you again, this time you gaze upwards and allow all of your concentration to be on the majestic bird that is doing circles in the air above. A huge wing span that is made up of so many browns and blacks you recognise this noble hunter immediately. Then your attention shifts just a little further afield as you notice another.

Two buzzards hunting together, both looking out for the same prize, both working as a team. You let out a little chuckle of both humor and sarcasm, if only your parents had done the same thing on this hill then maybe Pete wouldn't have broken his leg. Maybe he wouldn't have had the limp he has had for the rest of his life. Maybe, just maybe he would have then accepted that pint on the summer evening in the Tap and Spile.

You shake your head in a sobering fashion, pushing those deep dark memories back to the basement of your subconscious and focus on the land around you, the beautiful, wild scenery that stretches out before you in every direction. Whilst you've been daydreaming the landscape has gotten a little rougher, a little more rural. The grass is polluted by sheep droppings, manure left as a reminder from the hundreds of hill sheep that call this home, before their young are brutally taken and slaughtered, throats slit by a rusty knife as the life force slips from them. A far cry from the gorgeous oil painting existence that they had previously known. Some of the dung is fresh, some of it looks as if it has been there for years. Some of it doesn't even look as if it has come from sheep. Bigger, flatter moons of turd litter the grass, clearly from a bigger species, clearly from cows.

A huge shudder vibrates down your spine, as the thought of cows reminds you of the dream you had last night. You were alone in a deep dark corridor that sloped downwards, water came up to your ankles and the place was deadly silent, until the bull came.

An orange fungus has grown on the older specimens and thinking back to the slug from earlier you wonder just what tiny organisms are living on both the fungus and the dung itself. Nature's little miracles all living their lives the way they have too, every single one serving a purpose in the bigger, wider, vaster picture.

Ahead there is an old fence, partly standing, partly fallen, a real decrepit sight. Something that once stood so proud and provided the boundary that couldn't be crossed, imposing and vital but now verging on useless since the decay set in. Old sheep's wool sticks to the rough nails that protrude at various intervals, draped there like some ancient flags showing the full nature of the beings that have come and conquered that land and taken it for their own. The flags are dirty and torn though, almost as weather beaten as the fence itself. It's a long time since the victorious armies left them there. It makes you realise again where you are, turning three hundred and sixty degrees to take in a panoramic view around you, your solitude becomes apparent to you once more.

You press on, heading up, moving towards your goal and leaving everything else behind. Like so many other times in your life you are on your own in the middle of nowhere, but today you miraculously have a little fight and determination, you must push on and reach the summit.

Up above you can hear flowing water. Running faster than the stream that ended yours and Pete's friendship, but certainly not as fast and furious as the Niagara Falls.

You scurry up a small rise in the landscape, pushing your way through a small gauze like shrub, watching carefully so the spiky branches don't spring back and scratch your face. A task easier said than done, as each needle is desperate to pierce your skin and impale you with nature.

In the end you close your eyes and push your arms out and forcefully wade your way through. Suddenly you are standing overlooking a brook, with your toes are on the edge of a ten foot drop! You slam your anchors on, the horror of Pete's fall floods back into your mind, the sight of the broken bone sticking out playing over and over again. A few rocks fall heavily down from the edge on which you stand, evicted by the toes of your boots and splash without a trace into the crystal blue stream. Enchanting in appearance and almost a lure into harm, the lack of a splash back shows that the water is maybe deeper than you thought from here, that acknowledgment means your dig your heels in even further, desperate to hold on.

Your head is spinning a little, more out of shock at the sudden descent that greeted you through the brush, but also at what lies at the bottom of the drop below!
You look all around, wondering if there is any form of crossing. There is not. However, to your left there is a little ledge, approximately about 4 foot down. It's about five or six foot wide, and maybe another four feet in depth. You shift along to a little slope that heads towards the ledge and sinking down onto your backside you slide down and almost drip onto the ledge.
It's incredible that just such a little drop could change your whole perspective but doing that certainly has. You feel that despite there being a six foot drop still, you could lean down and touch the water that is beginning to sparkle in the clearing fog.
You steady yourself and sit down, holding the rock that is your base as if your life depended on it. You settle and for a second you relax. It is beautiful here. You are literally floating, sitting on a magic carpet made of rock and earth, suspended above both land and sea, a very special and unique place to be.
You peel your backpack from your body warmer and open the zip to reveal a shiny silver flask. Unscrewing the lid, your mouth begins to water at the thought of a caffeine top up, enthusiastically you pour a small amount into the metal lid, then you begin to relax further.
It really is beautiful here, a place hidden unless you seek it, an angelic haven that only you know about. You had mentioned it to her over the years. In your mind the area that had had such a huge influence on your childhood since your eighth birthday had also been a pivotal point of you growing up. You'd always wanted to return and in her you thought you'd found the perfect person to share it with. This place was your own private wonderland, but she came into your life and left it again without her ever getting the chance to be Alice.
Deep down you still don't know why she left. You did all you could to provide, worked all the hours you could, pushed for promotion, but it wasn't enough. Nothing was ever enough for her.
You take a sip of the steaming coffee you poured from your flask, Alta Rica your favourite, the caffeine instantly kicking in to give you a little buzz. She loved your coffee, you loved sharing it

with her. You always made coffee for the two of you in the morning. Every single morning you drank it together watching the day break, every single morning.

You can still remember the pain you felt when she turned around and walked out of the door without a word. You'd never really trusted her new boss anyway, but really thought everything you had was special. You'd created this life between you but now she was walking away leaving you with the home that was just too big for only you and had really stretched you further financially than you should have been. Her boss and his wife had even come around for a meal, she prepared and cooked it all by hand herself, refusing your offer of help. You'd been so proud that night, proud of your home and proud of her. Then he took her away.

Gazing into the brook, your eyes picking out single pebbles and watching them make their way down the rough and ready river bed, a tear begins to run down your cheek. You flick it off your face with the back of your right hand watching as it joins millions of other droplets flowing towards somewhere else six feet below you. Part of you moving onto a new life and leaving you behind stranded on this ledge.

Taking the flask lid you make a move as if to tip the entire contents down your throat, like a business man would a glass of bourbon after loosening his tie once he has returned home after a stressful day at the office.

The memories have turned the coffee sour though and instead of downing the caffeine infused shot, you toss it over the edge into the brook. The brown liquid mixes with the crystal clear for a split second, then it's gone. Absorbed by the world around it the colour melts into everything else. Just like you and her, gone and never to be seen again.

Quickly putting your flask away into your back pack, you stand up on that ledge and for a minute you pause. There is just a split second when you wonder what would happen if you jumped? Then your brain races you back to Pete, and instead you pull yourself up onto the outside world above. Leaving behind all your memories and thoughts, hoping that like your tears and coffee they have been washed away forever. If only it was that easy, maybe then you could leave her behind.

Back in the real world you again look around. You need to somehow find a way to cross the magical world you have just left behind. You heart tugs to the left, so that's the way you set off. Proving your ticker to be a great navigator you are quickly justified in your decision, just up ahead a small stone bridge crosses over the brook, covered in a small simple purple flower that is clearly native to these parts, but looks so beautiful as it comes into view from a distance.

As you cross you glance down, the water runs even faster than it did just a little bit further away, it makes you wonder exactly how far from here your coffee is. You continue on leaving the little brook, ledge and bridge behind.

Stepping over a minefield of mole hills you progress up the hill, the mist has gone now, leaving behind a beautiful blue autumn sky. Fresh and full of chill, the sun is beginning to shine but such is the time of year no real heat is given off. Instead its glow casts an ambient hue across such a barren landscape.

Despite the lack of direct heat, the weight of your back pack and the feathers inside your body warmer means you build up a little sweat as you plough forward. That's what you like to tell yourself anyway. It certainly has nothing to do with the frozen meal for one Jalfrezi you had last night. Nor is it anything to do with the six cans of Cobra lager you consumed along with it. In fact, come to think of it six is probably a conservative estimate, it was at least eight. An almost nightly occurrence since she left.

A little further in front you see a couple of big black birds busily pecking at something on the ground. Not the friendly little black birds that would quite happily take bird seed from your garden table, but two huge birds black in colour. Ravens you think but before you can really get close enough to see they turn and look at you casting a disgusted look in your direction and then fly off. Sitting on the posts of a half collapsed fence they watch until you pass the rotten lamb carcass they were feeding on.

You pause for a moment as you pass the corpse, although there isn't a great deal left other than bones and a little abandoned wool. It's fresh and new whiteness engulfed by the greyness of death and the decay of time.

So young with its whole life left to live, but now gone, nobody knows or cares. Left to die out here alone, as you walk away your whole body shudders as you suddenly realise that lamb could turn out to be you.

As you leave the ravens return, their day resumes but for the lamb it means its existence has even less evidence. One day there will be nothing to show it even existed.

There a something about the smell up here that makes you feel humble, humble and safe. The warm scent of the Heather, the earthy smell of the sheep dirt and mole hills, it all smells so natural. You feel liberated, for the first time in a long time your lungs and nasal passage feel clean, pure. Away from the constant infection and pollution that fills and surrounds your body in the city you were born, raised grew up and now work in. The very same city you have grown to detest and blame.

The mist is now long gone, whilst the air is still crisp, blue skies now reign. You continue to head up, trying to absorb every inch of the nature around you. A rabbit sticks its head into the air not far away to your left, its nose twitching at a high rate as it tries to work out whether you are friend or foe. Of course, it's the first, but as you keep your distance the rabbit decides it's not worth the risk of finding out and hops off to find another piece of grass to chew on. Who knows, maybe the grass is even greener over there.

The grass may be greener? How many times has that phrase had an influence in your life? So many it's hard to pick out the ones that are most prominent, however here you are still on your own. No partner, family you never see and a job that is nothing more than a habit. So, you ask out loud "is the grass greener Mr Rabbit?"

Obviously, your question receives no reply, instead the creature deposits small balls of muck on the green grass before hopping off out of sight to pastures new. The grass is always greener to him at least.

You've never been up this hill as high as this before, at least not that you can remember. None of it looks familiar and pedestrian traffic up here is so rare a little path has been carved through the tough clumps of grass, making navigation of a route so much easier. However, with the path there doesn't come any hazard signs and on a couple of occasions you nearly end up flat on your face as you trip on the rounded stones that pop up every now and then hiding under grassy knolls. Each and everyone could tell you its own story on how it got there, and indeed why it's there, but for now you are convinced that the reason for every single one of them is nothing more than to trip you up, to stop you reaching your destination. To stop you making your way to the top.

The summit of the hill is in sight now and as you climb nearer its peak the body of nature's creation makes it gradually more and more difficult by increasing the gradient.

But you are nearly there, on your own you have very nearly made it. A little sense of achievement begins to fill your heart with pride and spurs you on. A sensation that disappeared from your feelings the day she left. Nothing replaced pride, just a huge black gaping whole where it used to be.

Your mind begins to race away with itself and you begin to wonder what you will see when you get there. You picture things like flags of victory from long past climbers. All different colours and from different countries maybe?

An information sign highlighting all the points of interest that you can see from the wonderful three hundred and sixty degree view that will surround you?

There could be anything up there. The skeleton of a once famous explorer, still sitting there in his out dated clothes with a rolled up treasure map grasped in his boney fingers. He just never quite made it to his fortune, which means it could still be up there just waiting to be discovered...

With that thought you step out a little faster, eager to reach your destination and see what awaits you. You really hope it is the map and the treasure, even now this place brings out the kid in you.

Nothing else is in your mind now, your pace increased, your focus channeled ahead and upwards. You pass a huge boulder to your right and although the burning sensations in your calves tell you they yearn for a seat; your head tells them to keep moving. You are nearly there.

You follow the little path to the left and then it seems to jut suddenly to the right, avoiding a crater littered with wool from sheep that have used its natural shape to shelter from the elements, before one more little rise leads you out to the top.

Nothing lies ahead of you now, everything and everybody is below you. You are on top of the world.

Looking around you though your heart begins to sink as disappointment begins to set in. Yes, there are the fantastic views you expected, but there are no signs, no flags, no skeletons holding treasure maps, indeed there is no treasure at all. Nothing but tufts of grass and clumps of heather greet you, like there has been all the way up. Whilst you wanted to do this alone, you had hoped there would be some sort of evidence those great climbers before you had also conquered this peak, meaning that you had joined an elite crowd.

You stand there with your mobile phone in your hand ready to take a selfie to record this incredible moment, but as you realise that you actually had no choice but to come on your own, you put it away again. Who could you send it to anyway?

Sinking to your knees you begin to weep. How did you ever end up so lonely? You push yourself back into a lying position and gaze into the sky above you, grey clouds have begun to win the battle with the blue sky. You stare at them for a second or two, seeing different shapes appear and disappear as the clouds move east, then you close your eyes. You are slipping.

There is a beautiful rose cast to the sky when you wake, the sun is so distant now, as it starts to play a game of hide and seek with the moon behind neighboring hills. Everything has a pink tinge and the temperature has dropped to below nippy!

You stand up and straighten your body warmer, you must have been asleep for hours, the best rest you have had for months, just not where you wanted it. Picking up your back pack you slide the zip and pull out a woolly beanie hat. Slipping it onto your head you wonder how you have slept for so long and glancing at the sinking sun from the same level for the last time, you turn and start to head back down hill.

You must get back before it gets dark for your own safety, your mind reminds you of the poor lamb who was sacrificed to the elements, but really there is no rush. Nobody is at home waiting for you and there is nothing to go home for.

NO MERCY

MERRY CHRISTMAS

The first Christmas without her is definitely the hardest. The agonising build up of everyone bursting at the seams to tell you what they are planning to do, the pretentious bullshit of families who never see each other coming together to show solitude and to pretend to care. You on the other hand have nothing and nobody fucking cares.

At work you have to put up with the competition of seeing whose partner is getting them the most expensive present, eventually mastering the knack of switching off and putting all your concentration into anything else that enters your pickled, bitter and angry mind. Anything else but Christmas, please, anything else but this ridiculous charade of happiness.

The works party came and went. You didn't attend. The works Secret Santa came and went, you didn't partake, when the fake exercise of handing out the Christmas cards came about you sent none. You received very few anyway in return and even the ones you got weren't personalized with your name on, just 'Merry Christmas' from Laura, or Jack, or the man in the moon for all you fucking cared.

At home no tree went up, no decorations, no bright lights. What do you have to light up anyway? You are on your own in the dark. The path you have chosen has led you to somewhere so desolate that it reminds you of that hill you climbed as a child and went back to on your own when she first left. A narrow path set in its way. Nothing will make it venture in any other direction. Its destination set in stone and ground into the history of time, with only the one out come. Just like the path of your life. Everything positive and living cruelly taken by nature and the powers above, just like the little lamb you passed on your climb, defenceless and vulnerable, defeated and alone.

She never sent a card or a gift, or even acknowledged all your years together. Christmas's past was where so many memories were created, those Christmas's you looked forward too, believing things would get better. Special memories at a special time where alcohol, stars, giftwrap and cinnamon ruled. So many memories of the perfect time together, emotionally and physically. Now they were gone, pushed to one side, you are the last turkey on the shelf. The misfit that nobody wants to think about, the family secret hidden away, the work colleague that everyone else finds a little strange. You are totally fucked in existence and the future. Nothing can save you now.

Christmas Eve was the hardest; you could see everybody getting together in the local as you drove by. Spirits in fine fettle as the alcohol flows and people share kisses under the mistletoe. Couples hug and kiss each other as they enter and leave. It's one of the very rare nights that everyone is in such a good mood, never is there an argument or a fight, everyone simply loves being together and sharing the festive warmth.

You had a couple of invites to go out, but you just couldn't bring yourself to face it. The thought of you standing there alone was simply too terrifying. The black sheep amongst the pure and normal white ones, the loner that is different from the pack, the one on his own.

Instead you stay at home in the house you once shared with a bottle of blue sapphire gin replacing her for company. You don't even see past nine thirty.

The harsh reality of what you have lost hits the hardest at Christmas, of that there is no doubt. Her family has exiled you to non existence, even though she left you, with that discard comes the pain of losing more than one person you loved and thought of as your own family. They however have erased you from their minds, another morning passes and your letter box remains empty of Christmas cards. Empty that is other than bills.

You begin to drink more and more, stopping off at the nearest shop each night during the build up to the holidays for more alcohol. You move away from your favorites to whatever is the cheapest and on more than one occasion you use the saving in the price to double your purchase to two bottles. After all double will help you ease the pain even more, you will get through this difficult period quicker and once January finally comes around you will be able to go back to normality and have a few beers at the weekend only? Maybe you could even join a gym in the new year, tone up a bit? That might even help you move on from her and fill the huge crater she has left. Yes, a gym membership that would help in every way, you may even meet someone else. With that thought you pour another gin, but you never drink it, instead you crash out on the sofa still in your works clothes and again you think you see him.

You are not sure if you are dreaming or not, but it all seems so real that you are convinced that you definitely see him in the corner of the room, smirking with glee at your drunken demise. His huge horns filling the alcove next to the door that leads towards the kitchen, horns that look so fierce, as you stare you are sure you see dried blood stains on them, from some other sad bastard that he has dragged down and slayed. The deep, dull stain of the life source of something more vulnerable than you, marking this enormous creature like some kind of medal from a one sided battle of years gone by.

His deep, black hairy chest moves in and out as he inhales and exhales, his breaths seem to remove all the oxygen from the room until he breathes out again. You find yourselves gasping for air and trying to store as much of it as you can in your heavy lungs. Lungs that have started to feel the strain of your poor diet and constant drinking since the Christmas build up began, you sit on the sofa still in your suit and begin to gasp for air. Life choking away from you due to a lack of an available source to survive.

He says nothing and never moves, but in your mind he is getting closer. So close you can smell the putrid and earthy smell of rotten straw, the smell of a cow shed that has been left to foment for years, layer upon layer of waste entwined into the natural bedding, rotting together and decomposing at such a slow rate that the actual occurrence itself is almost made meaningless as it is taking so long. Still you can smell it and sense the decay. That along with the sickly sweet smell of the regurgitated cud on his breath.

His presence in your sitting room is so real, so intimidating. Standing right in the spot where you would have normally put up the Christmas tree. Ironically, he stands there as motionless as a downed pine, never moving just simply fixing his gaze on you.

You can't look him in his big amber eyes, glowing like the flames in the log burner that has long since gone out after being starved of fuel as your alcohol induced slumber kicked in.

Your eye's flit around the room, avoiding him at all costs, looking left then right, up then down, you avoid staring into those blazing eyes in case they drag you closer and devour you.

Then you see it, what your mind had wanted you to see all along, but the reasoning part of your brain had tried to avoid at all costs.

Stuck to his front right hoof is something shiny and red, the last embers from the log burner flicker and reflect in the tiny mirror it provides, the tiny mirror of a bow from a Christmas present.

You sit up with a start, still unaware if you are dreaming or if what you are seeing is real, leaning forward you stare directly at the bow. You have seen it before, but where? Red with tiny little silver dots on, so small that from a distance it looks like a perfect little crimson decoration that would top the perfect gift.

Then the penny drops, it's from the gifts you bought her last Christmas, the last one you shared together. Your memory digs deeper into the archives and provides you with an even more startling revelation, you can remember exactly which gift that bow was off, as the lady in the shop very kindly wrapped it for you.

The lady in the lingerie shop who joked that the wrapping paper and especially the bow matched the underwear within, red with tiny little polka dots on and very sexy.

You close your eyes, or are they already closed? Seconds tick by and you desperately try and chase the bull from your mind. When you reopen them you want him to be gone, more importantly you want that damned bow to be gone and with it the reminder of her.

Time waits for no man though and before you can fully chase the two of them from your mind you are quickly shaken by the shrill of your alarm clock. Your eyes snap open in sheer fear and panic, scanning every inch of the sitting room, but there is no sign of the bull or the bow for that matter. It's as if neither were ever there.

You throw yourself back into the sofa in relief, spilling the half full gin glass that is still in your hand over your suit trousers, both of which should have been taken away from the present situation before this happened.

"Fuck's sake" you mutter, standing to get a cloth.

Today is Christmas day.

HAPPY NEW YEAR

The rest of the holiday period disappears into oblivion with an ease you never thought would be possible. Your mobile never rings and there is a barren drought when it comes to invites to family events. There is however, always alcohol to keep you company and take the chill off your existence and the cold temperatures.

She was always big on the family thing at Christmas, as were her family. As the holiday week after Christmas powers on you start writing an imaginary diary in your head. Boxing day you would be at her mothers, the day after you always had a trip south to visit the aunts and uncles, then the big day usually bang in the middle of the festive period when everyone from far and away descended on her brother's house.

He always put on quite a show, from activities for the kids, to a feast fit for a king and catering for all dietary needs and tastes. A buffet that broke all the rules and exceeded every 'help yourself' meal you'd ever had the privilege of being invited too. Christmas at her brother's house was like a real royal occasion and one that was written in folklore in her family.

This year though your phone didn't ring with the usual invite, you weren't told "no it's fine honestly, we have everything sorted" when you asked if there was anything you could bring or help with. This year you were left to rot on your own, stewing in your own mental turmoil at trying to readjust whilst living on pot noodles, crackers and the just 'in date' biscuits you found left over from last Christmas. Stashed deeply and darkly on a shelf at the back of the kitchen cupboard where she used to keep her favourite treats and things. Before desperation set in over your alcohol fused refusal to go outside into the world to shop, you never even knew this shelf in your cupboard existed.

She had always wanted to put on a family event like her brother, way back from before she had even met you, but it never happened. There was always some reason or excuse from someone to say that they couldn't travel so far or that the child was ill. Her brother always stepped in though and somehow made everything alright. He really should have had a job working as a negotiator for some farfetched government organisation with a goal of keeping world peace, as that's exactly what he always seemed to manage. Everyone was able to attend when the function was switched to his house, probably because they knew his buffets were just too good to miss.

You never knew if she held that against you, her family's rejection of your perfect little home, but every Christmas time played out the same and resulted in you ending up elsewhere. Never was a family event held at your house, never was the family pulling crackers around your dinner table, it was always somewhere else, every single Christmas time.

By the time the 30th of December comes around you have almost lost the will to live. You long to be back at work so you can at least have the pleasure (if you can even call it that) of human company. A bizarre feeling really, causing a sickening, dull feeling in your stomach, you hate each and every one of them but now you are longing for the people that you despise being in the same room with every other week of the year, now the Christmas holidays are here you realise how much you miss those very same people. Right now, at this point in your life they are all you have. Fuck, how sad is that?

Your family left you behind a long time ago. No big quarrel, no big fall out, just four people going their own separate ways. You lost contact with your sister years ago when she got the chance of that big promotion in London. Although so many years have passed since she last listened to the latest heart throb on her walkman, moving to the big city gave her the opportunity to chase her dreams and at least be in the same city as the rich and famous. She never joined them of course, nor once did she ever doubt the decision to move. You left the equation very quickly and despite the occasional email you never really felt you knew what she was doing or who she even was anymore. Just somebody you used to know and had moved onto bigger and better things without you.

Your parents both remarried eventually and like a couple in their early twenties they both submerged themselves in their new partners and their families. You couldn't really blame them, they had new exciting lives to live, but the abandonment hurt and over time you became resentful.

These holidays saw you begin to drink more and more. Very quickly it moved on from a pleasurable tipple on an evening to the very first thing you thought of when you woke up. Not a need to drink or an addiction, simply a way to take away the pain and to try and help you forget how miserable and lonely your life had now become. Here you were, after everything you'd been through in life, alone. Alone and with no obvious route out of the darkness, there was no apparent way back from the hole you now found yourself in. Your whole world seems black; everywhere you looked you were either forgotten about or rejected. Nobody wanted you or wanted to be near you, looking at what you have become could you honestly actually blame them?

It is during a heavy drinking session on New Year's Eve that the penny finally drops and you realise through a lager and gin tinted vision that the common denominator in all of this is you. Every single person in this web of despair is connected by you.

Leaning forward you put your glass down on the table, you quickly reposition it to one side to make room for a virtual map that you begin to translate from your own mind. Pointing at nothing on top of the mahogany side table you start to imagine the faces of everyone you have loved and lost, everyone who has had the misfortune to enter your sad and desperate life, but then also have the fortune to walk away from you and out of your shallow existence. The map seems to get bigger as you start to remember more names of the people that have built you up before they let you down, or have they? Maybe after all of this time you begin to fully understand the full scenario, only now do you see that you are the one that let them down. You are the mercenary in all of this and it's so clear now, now that you have realisation and are finally able to embrace it.

The map gets bigger and bigger, in your mind the table is beginning to look like a page from one of the old road atlases' your dad always kept in the glove box of the family car and only came out on those very rare family days out, way before satellite navigation was even thought of. Usually after a full scale argument of whether you were lost or not!

The road to each individual character begins spreading like veins across tight skin, leading to another then another and all the time they connect because of you. You place your hand around the rim the gin glass, trembling as you make sure you have a tight grip. You pause for a second, tears beginning to flood down your cheeks, why has it taken you so many years to work it out?

You wipe your face with the back of your other hand and slowly pick the glass up with the other. You have no idea of your intentions other than to make the glass symbolise you in the centre of the map. You are the spider in the middle of the web, waiting to catch the flies. However, in this web there are no flies to catch, they've already escaped and flown away. Your hand shakes spilling a little Gin onto the surface, inside your mind is still flashing all the names of people that you have lost, displaying them like some kind of flashing neon notice that moves too fast for anyone to read, a really badly edited movie credit. The only thing that fits with both is that you are nearing the end. You move the glass to the centre of the table, holding it so it hovers about six inches above the wood. Then with all of your might you slam the glass into the centre of the table.
It smashes sending shards flying up through the air. Your hand and wrist follow through from the slam forcing the towering remains of crystal to rip into your flesh, tearing and splitting your skin in dozens of places. You don't feel a thing, you've had far too much alcohol for that, but you do notice the blood. Tears flood down your cheeks as you watch the crimson life force spray from your limb and soak into the carpet and the wallpaper. It's as if every drop represents a person from your imaginary map, every drop lost from your body indicates someone lost from your life, but they are all doing one thing in common, running away from you and trying to escape.
The clock on the mantelpiece has blood splattered across its glass face, hiding some of the digits behind the hands. You are staring right at it when the chimes make you jump a little signaling another hour gone. This time however it is signaling midnight. End of a day, the start of another and for tonight only, the end of a year, beginning of another.
Sitting alone, blood splattered up the walls and across the floor, the very life source that makes you exist spurting from your being whilst you are too drunk to control it, is how you see in the New Year.

JANUARY

The start of the New Year does nothing to lift your spirits, your mood and life continues in the same vain as it did the previous year and matches the stereotypical view of the first month of the year itself, miserable, grey and dank. The weather, like you, is beginning to fall.
You return to work with your hand, wrist and forearm bandaged but nobody asks you what you did to sustain the injuries. You're not surprised, you didn't expect them too. Nobody gives a fuck about you in that place. In fact, you would have been more surprised if somebody actually had asked or shown some concern.
It had taken about three days for the bleeding to finally stop. You quickly went through all the bandages you had in the house, moved onto hankies and then eventually toilet roll. Thankfully the day to return to work came just as the final roll was about to run out and, after purchasing a whole load more bandages from the little Boot's store at the railway station on your way in, you are able to change the dressing for something more hygienic. Paying well over the odds, even you know the importance of not going into work with bloody tissue paper wrapped around hand.
Quickly nipping into the toilets in the station you take off your coat and suit jacket. It is so cold this month too, another word that could sum up how you feel about your existence, so damned cold. Bitter and cold, emotionally and physically.
Once the suit jacket is off you notice the blood is already beginning to seep through the sleeve of your white shirt.
"That's one for the bin" you say under your breath as you undo the cuff link and roll the sleeve up to your elbow, quickly glancing at the old man who has just entered and stood at two urinals down. You stare at him for three o four seconds before deciding that he definitely didn't hear you. Convinced you turn back to face the tiles before looking back to your arm. The toilet tissue has begun to stick to the open wounds so much that you have to use your finger nails to pull bits of rogue tissue out, stinging with every touch.
You really should have gone to hospital, but you just couldn't face it and too be honest you were never sober enough to get yourself there. Most days you'd change the 'dressing' and then get so drunk you'd forget about it till you woke up on the sofa at

some unearthly time. The first couple of times you drifted off you woke with big red patches on the cushions where the blood had seeped through, but you did nothing about it. Instead you started laying towels over the cushions. You didn't even try to clean the stains. You could always buy new ones you kept telling yourself as you poured yourself another drink, or you could even buy yourself a new sofa you thought, chuckling out loud as you rested back onto the sofa you currently owned. When the short lived burst of laughter subsides, you take the tumbler full of whiskey up to your mouth and down it all in one.

It's those early January days back at work that make you notice that you no longer talk to people. It's not just the work colleagues that you never liked anyway, but people in general. The lady in the newsagents one dinnertime tried to engage in the usual polite conversation about the rain that was pouring down outside whilst you both waited in line to be served. You had nothing to come back with; absolutely no words entered your head, your communication skills now rendered obsolete. Instead you simply nodded and turned the other way, fidgeting with the chocolate bars to try and look busy as if deciding which one you want. Thus, avoiding any further conversation. Maybe she is battling her own demons and feels she just needs to talk, but when she continues to talk to you informing you "that this rain is here to last at least until the middle of the next week" it all becomes too much. You don't say anything out loud you simply leave your place in the line, even though you are up next, place the bottle of lucozade back in the fridge and walk out.

Your head is pounding with both anxiety and anger. Why did she have to pick you to talk too? Why couldn't she have bored the old lady behind her with her weather forecast? And how the fuck does she know what the weather will be like in over a week's time? Those jumped up tarts on the telly can't even get that right and they have the benefits of satellites and all sorts of technology!

You look at your watch trying to decide what to do. The next shop is a good five minutes' walk away and you really don't have time to get there and back. You could of course just stand outside and wait for the woman to leave but that just fills you with dread. What if she decides she wants to tell you February's forecast whilst she's on a roll, so instead you decide to just head back to the office through the sleet without the sugary drink. The remainder of the hangover has won for the day, but you'll be back tomorrow for a pick me up after another night drowning your increasing sorrows, of that you are certain.

THE FOG

The fog is all around, engulfing everything and everyone, if indeed there actually is anyone else out there. The damp, fuzzy aura swamps your senses, filling your eyes, mouth and nostrils with grey, completely saturating you and taking your breath away.

Is there anyone else out there? Is there anything else out there?

Grey, nothing but grey. Grey and damp, is this the world you have finally been delivered too? The path that you have ran along without any control has brought here, you were always destined to be heading here, so is this the existence you now need to accept?

You walk a little further timidly, your head tilted downwards towards the ground below. You concentrate on your steps and try and navigate your way across the clumps of green grass that provide a contrasting carpet of colour to the dank mist all around, the mist that has you surrounded and has swallowed you up.

You don't know where you're going, or even which direction you are heading, but you move forward. What is the use in going backwards? You can't change what went on there or who is there. You can't change the plot that has brought you here, this path was mapped out for you a long time ago.

This is where you were always intended to be. You were meant to be here in the murky abyss with no outlet, there was nothing you could do to prevent this, you were always due to fall and now, into the fog you have finally fallen.

Your life choices have clearly had an influence, but ultimately this is where you belong. In a huge great nothing, that leads to nothing. Which is all you have ever been, nothing.

You let out a little cough as the fog tickles the back of your throat. The aftershock makes you miss your step slightly and in doing so you pause for a second battling to keep your balance.

The clumps of grass are getting thicker and more uneven, the green getting more emerald like in the ambience, casting an Irish tint over everything around. You stay still for a second gazing at the floor, each blade jutting out like a little piece of wire waiting to trip you up. Each wire leading to a landmine of explosives that could take you down and bring about your final demise. Each wire potentially the one that could finally blow, the explosion to end it all.

Shaking your head to eliminate the thought from your mind you look back to the horizon. Particles of mist hang and dance in front of your eyes as if each and everyone is doing a little show for you and trying to entice you to follow them.
"Follow me, follow me" they say as they try and encourage you into one of their strategically placed honey traps.
All the same but all making different journeys, the fact you are all here together has to mean something. You, the grass, the sprite like moisture particles, something has drawn you all here together and at this very moment in time.
You walk on, your hair beginning to stick to your forehead on flesh that is new to this outside world as recently your hair has started to recede as well as displaying a silvery grey sheen. You feel small droplets run from your weathered skin, creating a liquid mask that is hiding the real fear that lurks underneath.
The mist that surrounds you seems to be getting thicker the more absorbed you are into nowhere. The ghostly hue invites you in deeper, lures you to venture further and penetrate its glistening walls. You continue to walk.
You're not cold as you walk, despite the damp. In fact, if anything the atmosphere around you and the particles that rest on your body leave you feeling warm, too warm if anything, almost uncomfortable. Your body begins to feel clammy and uneasy as if you are nervous or as if somebody has put the central heating on during a very warm summer afternoon and then made you sit there fully clothed with your body temperature rising. The heat invading you like a virus, until..... Exactly? until what?
Dank, dark and miserable, the earth begins to become you. You are beginning to mirror the environment that is trying to consume you, you are becoming lost in the world where you once existed. You have fallen so far, so deep, there can be no way back for you now.
Maybe that's the whole point. Maybe this is where you belong? Lost on the foggy moors alone and not belonging to anyone. Fallen with no one to catch you. Left here to rot and fester, a perfect meal for a million different critters who need you to survive. On your knees and defeated until all the bugs strip your body of every ounce of value and worth.

You are nothing but a mere morsel at the bottom of the food chain now, like a creature that has been lurking at the bottom of the ocean for centuries, you have been washed all the way to the surface for the world to see your hideous form. In the change of environment and exposure to the real world you have drowned. Drowned in your own emotions, drowned in your own self pity and left to wallow. Nothing but food for the parasites. Maybe after all that was your purpose? You were put on this earth to struggle, to mean nothing, then when the time was right, even that existence was taken away from you. Your lifeline crushed like a spider under foot.

Tricked into believing you had a purpose and tricked into meaning you were something, you tried to make the most of life, but you now realise that you were wrong.

You used to be a sweet boy, a considerate lover and a passionate man, believing in yourself and your role amongst others. You knew the difference between right and wrong, had morals that you dedicated your life too. You could have had family if lady luck had dealt you a different hand and you would have made a great dad, of that you are certain.

You would have given anything to have had a son or a daughter to raise and show the world. A family to show the right path too, then make sure they stayed on it. A family to make you proud, quite simply the family to replace the one you no longer have. You always wanted that, a family unit like when you were younger. However, you wouldn't make the same mistakes, you would be different. With a family you wouldn't be on your own now. With a family you wouldn't be here now in this desolate place. Maybe, just maybe, with a family to look after you would have survived, maybe you would have even made it.

You wouldn't be this pathetic creature ambling along in the fog on your own, heading towards oblivion with no direction, no passion or fight. A broken man, facing your fate on your own, staring down the barrel of a very murky and non-descript gun. You are no longer even worthy of a decent execution.

Except you aren't alone, up in front there is something else. There is another being, breath puffing into the air before you at a rate and rhythm that indicates both coolness and composure.

This is a creature that is comfortable with its existence; this is the force that has brought you here.

He has been watching you all along, all through your life and now he has you. Alone and vulnerable, you are his.

Your head is hanging both in shame and exhaustion; you stumble and end up on your knees with your face almost engulfed by coarse and rigid blades of knife sharp grass.

You slowly lift your head and your eyes fix on the plumes of hot air that cuts through the fog like a knife through butter. They follow the trail and your face begins to feel the warmth of another's breath, the further towards the sky your face rises.

Whoever is standing in front of you is clearly huge, huge and magnificent in their own right, huge and the most powerful being you have ever encountered.

Tilting your head slowly upwards you follow the trail of breath and as you begin to stand and stretch to your full capacity you try your best to go face to face with the beast that has the audacity to survive out here. Your whole body shudders in realisation. You know exactly who this is.

A huge ring vibrates in his nostrils as he takes deep and measured breaths, his huge black nose glistening with the dewdrops of the fog, but also with the vibrancy of the life force that oozes from within. This creature is magnificent and intimidating, beautiful and terrifying all at once. He is not here because he has fallen, unlike you. He is here because he is the reason you have fallen!

The huge bull stands head and shoulders and then some above you, even when you are fully stretched. He is everything you are not, everything you aspired to be. Perfection in existence, purity and determination in a bodily form, power and beauty personified. You kneel at his feet, like a captive ready to be beheaded. You have submitted and given in to the dark and evil power that has hunted you.

The amber of his eyes glow like flames in the miserable hue, he is vibrant and alive, his black fur shines like the stars above, the pale pink indentations of his flared nostrils reflect like the moon. He is the world, he is the universe and he has finally come for you.

THE DEEP
BLUE SEA

You park the car at the far side of the car park, as far away from the entrance as you can but also as near to the cliff edge as physically possible, just in case you decide to go through with it. In your boot you have three metres of garden hose, which you cut from the green and grey reel by the shed before you drove here. You have no idea of any scientific method, other than just shoving it up the exhaust pipe, then through a narrow gap in the driver's window, before turning on the ignition.

In the glove box you have two litre bottles of Whiskey and around a hundred or so tablets of various pain killing drugs. All just to help numb the pain and give you Dutch courage. Just in case you don't have the courage to drive off the cliff.

The area is deserted apart from one car in the corner adjacent where a young couple are making out in the back seat. Through the steamed up window you can just make out her silhouette as she rides him slowly and firmly, the car rocks slightly in rhythm of their love making.

You can remember the days that would have been you, as a sharp dagger of jealousy rips through your heart making you gasp a little for breath, but not enough to take life from you. You have done more than your fair share of fucking in cars, one night stands, people committed elsewhere and girlfriends who enjoyed the added excitement of being seen.

The rain is falling in the direction from the sea, cold and salty it splatters on your windscreen with a petulant slap, slap, slap. Turning off the ignition the wipers stop and within two seconds you have to switch it back on again to clear the wet shield that has taken over the glass and distorted your vision of the deep blue sea, salty water has taken over your world completely. Whether it be the ocean induced rain or the tears you seem to have been spilling for months.

The mechanical swoosh of the wipers joins in with the slapping of the heavy rain, then your windscreen begins to steam up too, so you put the fan on which instantly adds to the orchestra of unwelcome noise. You wonder if the lovers in the other car are having the same difficulty, or even if they can hear the noise of the rain above the moans and groans of them screwing each other's brains out.

You shake your head, what are you thinking? They're fucking not reading a weather forecast and as you tut in disapproval at your own thoughts your heart sinks just that little bit deeper with realisation and jealousy. Once again you remember the days that would have been you and wonder just when did you become so old and cynical? When did your life descend from back seat adventure to being here ready to take your own life.

Seagulls soar and circle up a height in the dull grey sky. Squawking and talking to each other, your mind moves away from thinking about you and you begin to wonder what the seabirds are saying to each other. Are they planning they're next adventure across sea to lands new? Or are they talking about the best places to fish? Or maybe, just maybe, they are talking about you. Laughing at the lonely man sitting in his car, deciding whether or not he should kill himself and finally end it all. Who knows?

You watch for just over a minute and a half as they glide in circles over the cliff edge, amazed at how they stay in flight against the conditions. In relative terms each individual bird is minute compared to mother nature and the forces she throws at them, so small and against the world, just like you, only these birds are so strong and focused, so they survive.

The strength of the gulls is inspiring, but also humbling. It reminds you of why you drove here, why you needed to get some space and tranquility. It reminds you of how meaningless you have become in the big wide world and how meaningless the world has become to you. Unlike the seabirds, you have lost the will to live.

To the right of where you have parked, there is a dark grey waste bin with graffiti sprayed on all four sides. Its mouth is crammed full and overflowing with McDonald's cartons and drinks cans. Litter spills onto the concrete slabs below that have gone three or four shades darker with all the rain. Everywhere around you are surrounded by grey, salt and decay.

The paving, the sky, the sea, all grey today. Everything and nothing, a world that merges into one, one that means nothing. Nothing new or exciting surrounds the once thriving seaside, the whole environment is seedy and dour, a total let down to how you remember it as a kid.

You focus your attention back to the sea. That after all is why you came, the reason that you are here on such an uninviting day. The beautiful deep blue sea with the glorious shower of colours from the corals and fish life, a world full of life and so self sufficient that it needs no man, in fact man is the one that brings it harm. A wonderful place, almost a different planet and one that flourishes on its own and without the cruel resentment of the one you inhabit. No bitterness flows within, no anger and loneliness, no harm resides in blue endless mass, just pure and undisturbed nature.

The sea. Automatically you mind floods with images of creatures going about their business without pressure, floating almost motionlessly through the invisible currents, getting from the place they were to the place they need to be and leaving nothing more behind them than just a slight trail of bubbles. A simple but so effective existence, there and then gone in a second.

The sea has always fascinated you and scared you both at the same time for as long back as you can remember. Early trips to the seaside lead to you wanting to know more about the huge expansive alien world that began where your golden playground ended. Rock pooling was one of your favorite adventures, but you never caught any of the animals you found, you didn't even pick them up. You simply used to stare in wonder at something so different from you in such an alternative environment, different species so different to your own in a completely different world.

Then when you were about ten years old you were allowed to watch Jaws for the first time. The fact that something so mystical as the ocean could house creatures as huge and powerful as the Great White Shark added to the intrigue, a new passion that was as much about fear and respect as it was about desire to learn, took control and an infatuation with Sharks was born that day.

Wonder and fear, quite a complicated and conflicting view of something that controlled so much around the earth. The weather, access, a barrier, the deep blue sea and all that lived within, was everything to our existence. Without it the human race would cease to function. It really was the be all and end all.

You shuffle forward to the edge of your driver's seat to look at the wonder of the world that was currently about sixty feet below you. You are parked approximately three to four feet from the edge of the cliff, so by stretching forward you are close enough to see the back wash of the waves as they crash off the cliff base.

Hostile and aggressive the water sprays up into the air with so much force that you think it is trying to reach up and take you, drag you down through its white foamy spit and swallow you deep below, you'd be gone in a second.

Like so many childhood memories and obsessions, time has tainted your view and memories. The ocean that you are seeing now isn't that beautiful blue hive of life, teaming with rainbow coloured life forms, it's cold and dark and grey and empty. Your mind starts to wander away as your stare into the abyss and as it does the vision you have changes. Instead of the fish and coral you see used condoms and tampax floating near the surface, leaving behind a greasy residual trail of human discharge. You see plastic drink bottles bobbing in and out of the water like the corpses of dead men after a ship wreck and you see twisted, knurled branches and tree trunks that have been washed downstream and into the sea after some violent storm that probably did even more damage on land.

The sea that you are staring at is one to be feared, one of danger and one that wants to take you. Everything in it is dead. The sea itself is inky black and dying, still going through the motions of its daily routine out of habit.

Back and forth, back and forth, tide in, tide out. It's spirit completely worn down like the stones in carries, the ocean that you are staring so deeply into is tired. Tired and shut down, just like you.

You close your eyes and he is back. The bull, standing there with steam slowly sliding from his nostrils, he is looking straight into your eyes, beckoning for you to move the car forward.

"Come" he mouths at you, not making a single noise but that in itself is more daunting than him actually speaking.

"Move the car forward and take a swim with me."

You jolt upright in your seat, eyes as wide as saucers and glance down to see you hand on the key in the ignition, ready to turn it to start the engine. Startled you slam your foot on the brake pedal, even though the car isn't running, you push the pedal as hard as you can, so hard cramp shoots up your calf like needles.

You are beginning to slip again, slipping and falling deeper and he is showing you no mercy. You are there for the taking.

What if you had started the engine? Would that have been so bad? You gradually let your foot off the pedal and slink back into your seat. Maybe that's what you should do. Start the car up and put it in reverse. Back up as far as the car park will let you and then hit the accelerator as hard as you can, driving you forward with speed and power. Crashing through the fence that is there to stop people doing exactly that, you could really fly and be free.

You imagine how that must feel, hovering in the sky for a moment as if time has stopped still before hurtling downwards towards the end, before the huge splash that closes the chapter that is your miserable life.

Just before you hit the water you hear the bull laughing, a deep and loud boom of a laugh that makes you panic and feel sick at the realisation of what you have done, but by then it is too late.

You shoot forward in your seat again, eyes once more like saucers, your shoulders shiver as a cold dagger jabs right between them and down your spine in a mixture of emotions. He has nearly got you, you are so weak. If he ups his game just one more notch you will be his and gone forever.

Your eyes turn towards the glove box opposite the passenger seat. You know there is enough alcohol and medication in there that would send you into a long and endless sleep. Why don't you just lean over and take them? Open the bottles and swig the contents in three or four mouthfuls, you've done it before at home. Then open the sachets of pills. Pour them into your hands before you shovel them all into your mouth, swallowing as many as you can in huge gulps. You could then open the second bottle and, as you gulp the brown fiery liquid down, like you would fruit juice, you'd very quickly slip away.

The alternative of course, is to connect the hose and turn on the ignition. In fact, you could then do the decent thing by taking the pills and liquor too, double jeopardy but guaranteed results surely.

Pride, hurt, lost, alone, abandonment, hate, anger, love and sadness, the dagger twists them all around your spinal column, jabbing each and everyone into your most vulnerable points. The pain is so great you can't move or put up a fight, the emotions have paralysed you and left you defenceless. You are no longer day dreaming and the laughter from the bull is so loud and real that you are sure when you turn around to see if he is behind the car you will see him sitting there gloating in the back seat. So sure you are that your nostrils start to twitch sending a signal to your brain that you can smell his smell, the aroma of rotten hay and silage, like you did at Christmas.

Instead you see the young couple are still fucking, going a little faster. In the few seconds you look her tempo is rising, at least one of them must be about to cum soon, maybe both.

Not wanting to witness that you turn back towards the sea. You need to do something, so despite the rain you open the driver's door and step out into the monsoon conditions.

Zipping up your coat and pulling up your hood you take a couple of steps forward and lifting your right leg first you cross the fence. Now nothing stands between you and the huge drop into the mystical world that has held your fascination since being a child. You really could end it now and nobody would give a fuck. The wind is stronger than you thought when inside the car and you position your feet apart to help keep you grounded. Nearer to the edge you can see more of the carnage that happens repeatedly at the foot of the very rock you're standing on.

The water crashes against cliff, the dishwater grey giving way to a frothy white spray that signals destruction and separation. Almost as quickly as it hits, the water pulls back and reveals the landscape underneath. Jagged and sharp boulders protrude the water looking like teeth from the jaws of the sharks that have fascinated you for so many years, then they are gone as another wave smashes over the top of them and into the huge wall that they were once part of. The great wall that you are standing on top of, it could all go crashing down at any moment, sending you hurtling down into the froth and abyss. Swallowed by the circle of life repeating itself over and over again, your demise would then be complete and totally natural.

The wind ripples through your jacket pushing you slightly forward. You gaze down at the death trap below, the sound of the bull's laughter still ringing in your ears. He is still behind you, urging you to fall further, deeper.

You could quite easily jump here, right now and nobody would know. He could quite easily push you over the edge, still nobody would know. It may take a few days before your body was washed back into shore. In fact, you read a story in the newspaper recently about a woman who had been swept away in strong winds and it had taken nearly six weeks for her body to finally come ashore and even then it was thirty miles down the coast. The salt water and animals feeding on her had taken such a toll that they were only able to identify her by her dental records.

You picture your lifeless body floating face down in the grey. Fish nibble at your decaying flesh, but not the beautiful blue and green and purple ones you imagined earlier, these are the ugly deep sea fish with jaws almost bigger than their heads and glazed huge eyes that are used to seeing nothing but the darkness of the bottom of the ocean. Monsters of the deep feeding on junk thrown into the sea from the world above, you have finally found your place in this world.

The rain seems to be getting heavier now, already your coat that claims to be waterproof is saturated and you can feel the damp, cold violation touching your skin through your clothes. You shiver again but this time due to nothing but the weather. As it turns out it could be the most important shake your body has ever done, as without even knowing what you are doing, your body diverts to self preservation and guides your tortured brain back over the fence and into the car.

Tears are flooding down your cheeks as your hands, white with the cold and wet, turn the key in the ignition. The engine roars into life instantly and instinctively you put the motor in reverse and move. Your decline has been happening for a long time now, but now you know how far you have fallen. The cold realisation that just seconds earlier you were so close to the end.

You pass the lovers on the way out of the car park. The car now motionless meaning a state of orgasm has been reached. You wonder for a split second if they would have been aware that whilst they were both ejaculating a suicide was taking place so close to them?

Hovering over the cliff where you were just standing the bull glares at your rear lights as you pull away out of sight. He very nearly had you there and he knows it. He could have given you the little nudge you needed, but that isn't the way his master likes him to work. The disgrace and embarrassment are in the fact the prey makes the decision to be caught. That is the fun of the chase and the hunt. He very nearly has you. He will not give up now.

SOLO SOLITUDE AND SOUL

You are alone. Completely alone in everything you do. Everyone else has gone, everyone you have ever loved has ran for the exit door, bolted. Left you, left here
Everyone you have ever opened up to or let into your life has disappeared without a trace. You are alone, operating solo.
Like a lone wolf you are living in solitude, doing all you can to survive and fend for yourself. Brave and taking everything life throws at you, it was only a matter of time before you were struck down. The pack was always going to be strong for you to fend off. Hurt too many times, your soul just doesn't have the strength to repair you again, to regenerate the skin that has been torn, to ease the mental torture they've put you through. The wounds go too deep, you are a wounded animal suffering and all that is left for you now is dying.
Dying alone.
A feeling you remember writing about all those years ago as you listened to your heroes on your Sony Walkman. Writing hoping that one day the world would read your words and change. Writing as if your life depended on it, now it really does.

Pointless.

Oh life, dear life,
Where have you gone,
What have I done,
To make you disappear,
And leave me 'Pointless' in your place.

But I live in hope, just in case.....

Oh life, dear life,
My dreams are all gone,
My dreams are all dead,
And now I've nothing left,
I'm just so 'Pointless' in this place.

But I live in hope, just in case.....

So never value life highly,

'Cause it's never really yours,
It's so easily snatched away,
From underneath your nose.

And that's so right, so so right.

Oh life, dear life,
Where have you gone,
What have I done,
To make you disappear,
And leave me 'Pointless' in your place.

But I live in hope, just in case.....

Nothing but a young teenager's emotion and certainly no Wordsworth but growing up these words meant something to you. How could somebody so young predict his own destiny? Unknown to you then, but now over thirty years later these words mean even more than ever.
For a long time, you have seen this coming. The vultures have been circling for long enough, but now even they seem to have lost interest. They have gotten bored with staring at your pitiful carcass and deserted you like everyone else. The prolonged agony of your miserable demise is even too much for life's most notorious scavengers. They have left you to rot, but they'll come back once you have finally gone and take what they want. That is of course if there is anything worth taking.
Feeding on what is left of the body that once had so many hopes and dreams, feelings and emotions, love and hate, all nothing now but fodder in waiting for vultures.
It won't be long now.....
"Not everyone has left you."
"Yes, yes they have!"
"No, they haven't, you just don't see. Your vision is fogged by the mist of your self-pity and hate. It blinds you."
"Look around there is no one here. Think back to what I had, where I was and who I belonged with. I have lost everything. Everyone has fucked off and left me. I have no one, I trust no one, and deserve no one."

"There is no such thing as trust. You can never, ever completely trust anyone, so that is not a valid reason for the state you are in. Alone yes, but not everyone has left you."

"Yes everyone!"

"No, not everyone! He still watches, he still waits, he still comes. He always comes. He's watched over you since the day you were born. Now you are very nearly his."

"What? Who? What are you talking about? Who watches over me?"

"The bull. He comes every night and watches you sleep."

"The bull? What the fuck are you on about?"

"Beelzebub. He has shown such a strong interest in you lately, but he's watched you since the sun shone on your head for the first time and since the first drop of rain landed on your tiny little head. Watching and wanting, waiting."

"Watching? Waiting? Wanting what?"

"Wanting you, he wants to take you. He is the only one that wants you."

"He wants to take me? Take me where?"

"Take you down, deep down into the dark."

"The dark? What's the dark?"

"It's where you are now. Only you're just on the outside, your journey is only beginning, but you will slip further. It was him that took you to the cliff top that day in the rain. Yet it was me that made you stop driving your car into the sea. It was me that stopped you jumping. It was me that saved you."

"The dark? Journeys? Slipping? You saved me? Are you mad? In fact, who are you anyway? Fuck I must be the mad one. Who the fuck are you!"

"Who am I? I am you."

"Me? Shit I am mad!" You look at the floor, eyes glazed in disbelief.

"Yes, you. The other side of you, the side that sees everything, the side that has watched you on this downward spiral since it began and hoped we would see our way out of it."

"The side of me that sees? Sees what?"

"The side of us that sees all that is us. Where we've been and where we are going, who we are and who we've been. I am you.

All we are and all we've become, I am our last chance, the final hope. I am trying to save me, us."

"I really am confused. You are me? A voice in my head?"

"No! Not a voice in your head! I am our voice, I am you. I have been going through all of your life, OUR life, trying to see where we went wrong. Looking at our memories and dissecting the effect that they have had on us. I've been trying to understand where we went wrong.

People say you can always remember where you are on pivotal days in history. The day JFK was killed, the day Princess Diana died. All huge days and everyone has a memory of them. It is the same with us. Every point of our life has been a 'pivotal day in history' only we haven't died yet!

I've seen you when take us shopping, stocking up on Paracetamol and Ibroprufen two boxes at a time. Storing them all in the bathroom cabinet that has been pretty much empty since she moved out and left us.

I know that you have been thinking about taking them all at once and washing them down with a bottle of whiskey. Taking our life away from us, killing us because you cannot go on. The past has killed everything we have ever dreamt of and the very spirit that drives us on. We are practically dead already.

I've been going through it all, looking at everything and the choices we have made. Our school memories, the time Pete broke his leg and gave us the first taste of rejection. The fun days we had when we didn't give a fuck about anything or anyone, we just drank and fucked."

"I think I've lost my mind."

"The exact opposite my friend. We have FOUND our mind. I've been remembering when we met her, how happy she made us, how she left and when she left. I've been going through everything we've lived through, trying to look for a way we could change something."

"Trying to change what? And if you're me how come I haven't been reliving those memories too?"

"Trying to change where we are heading too and then stop it. Trying to understand what put us on this road and looking for the way off it, an escape, but I don't think there is one. The part of us that you see as you hasn't seen it because you've been too busy wallowing in self-pity and hate. Always looking on the dark side and now it is too late for us. He will come and take us."

"He? The bull? What does he want with us?"

"Yes, the bull. He wants to destroy us and present our soul to his master. That's his job and he is an expert at it. He identifies the weak from birth and follows their progress and life all the way through, until they become so fragile that he can manipulate them for one last time. That's when you go. Everything in our life has happened for a reason and happened because of him. He has pushed us to where we are and now he will give us one final shove. One little nudge and down we go, hurtling into the dark. One for all and all for one."

DEPRESSION

There is a dark room somewhere in our subconscious. A room that is so shut off, lurking down a long and sinister corridor which lets in no light. No light and no warmth. Nothing can grow there, nothing positive abides there, nothing can live and prosper. Nothing of any good anyway.

The corridor to get to this room is dank, dark and rotten with a feeling of nausea and the scent of putrid decomposing masses, all of which have had the very life force sucked out of them on their damned journey to try and break the spell and beat the lure of the room. This is where he has taken us and we are alone.

In the far off distance there is a sound we are familiar with, one we have heard a hundred times before when we were young, a sound that we instantly recognise and open our heart too. The muffled crackle of a record player turntable airing the hidden secrets on the black vinyl disc it is spinning. We cannot make out the tune, only the beautiful sound of the turntable, Music captured in time and perfection. We know though where the link with us and tune has come from. Our instinct tells us it will be from one of the ex juke box seven inches we bought from Millers all those years ago at school. But why are they playing now and why here?

We stand still for just a split second, the water continuing to run past our feet. Dale Road, that's the link, the house on Dale Road with all the wheel trims and the Doctor that butchered his family. We used to go to Millers at dinnertime and buy those records, then on our way home we would always pass Dale Road and spend some time there. That was until we cooked up the courage to go and have a closer look that day. We ignored the obvious danger and trespassed into his garden, through the weeds and then peered through the big bay window. There was nothing much to see other than dead flies. Dead flies and all of those black alabaster bulls.

The music is still playing, only now there is another beat, almost drum like but playing a faster and more purposeful beat. It appears to be getting louder, getting nearer, a deep and intimidating drone that sounds like hooves, that's it. It sounds like the hooves of a huge bull pounding towards us, drowning out the beat of the music, even down here the bull is coming after us, pursuing us right until the end.

We are no longer standing still, as a rat runs past our feet, rubbing its manky flea ridden fur against our bare ankle. It instantly makes us want to reach down and scratch, but it is so dark down here our hands have to be our guide stretched out in front of us. Keeping us safe. We cannot let them leave our gaze for just a moment, or we may fall, then what? That could be the end of us, drowned in this disgusting, raging flow of sewage and shit.

The rat runs ahead, oblivious to both the contact and the vulnerable position it unwittingly put us in. It scurry's along the corridor spreading its germs and virus's without even knowing the catastrophic effect it is having, its fleas will have to take their own chances in finding a new host. Running ahead it knows where it needs to go, it has direction, it is heading for the door.

Behind the scurry of the rat we can still hear the hooves, way, way off. The bull is travelling with speed and zeal, the clatter of hooves getting closer and closer. The fear of him catching us pushes us forward, pushes us to where the rat is heading.

The door is daunting, black, solid and formidable. Made of wood thicker than most bricks, studs cast of iron that themselves defy the logic of history and time, hinges so big and gothic looking that the door itself portrays something so ghastly and scary we never ever want to reach it, but the corridor seems to drag us along deeper, like some sort of invisible escalator.

We are on it, on a journey and now there's simply no way off. Apart from the sound of the bull in the background drowning out the music, we are alone.

Approaching the door quicker than we want too, and with such purpose that for a second, we move our outstretched arms from in front of us to the sides to feel against the walls and gain composure. It may be our imagination, but the walls seem to be moving, growing closer together, forcing us along the corridor even quicker towards the door. Towards that daunting door.

Our feet seem to be somebody else's now, we don't control them. We are moving nearer and nearer to somewhere we desperately don't want to go, but we can't stop our self. It's out of our control. Our destiny hinges on arriving at that big, deep wooden portal and where it may take us. A journey into the abyss, a journey into the deep and dark unknown, a descent into the unknown. The

hooves behind us continue to get louder and closer. Somewhere in the distance is the high pitches shrill of some exotic bird, a bird of beauty or a bird of prey, either way its bellowing cry of warning reaffirms once again the danger we are in. This path of solitude cannot lead to anywhere pleasant.
The gradient of the path beneath our feet starts to sink, very much like the faith and trust we have in our heart and own destiny. Going lower and lower, water sloshes around our ankles, sending little shivers down our spine. Like so many things in our life before this demise, the water has been there all along. It's only when it's all around us with no way out do we notice that it is there, it is right below our feet always.
The water runs down hill, cloudy and contaminated, polluted and poison, running away with our feet. Rafts that simply flow with the tide, we have no control anymore, something else is taking us wherever they want us to be. We are spiraling down and out of our control, each step we take takes us further away from what we know, further from the light and into the darkness. The black and sound of running water consumes us, cancelling out everything we remember from before, and will ever know again. As we slide, we are alone.
Our journey to the door is nearly over, years and years it has taken us to get this far. Years and years of rejection and hurt for us to get so low, now we are nearly at the destination that was mapped out for us the day we were born.
The door is huge with its ominous mouth glaring down at us as we approach. The size of its entity looms above us, we cannot believe our journey is going to take us down to this monster of an entrance to somewhere that exists alongside the world we know. We automatically think of it as an entrance, but maybe it is an exit? We cannot say for sure, but our gut tells us there's more chance of it being the beginning of something dark rather than our chance to escape to the bright lights.
We can still hear the bull behind us, catching up and making us push on ahead. Majestic in his stride and determined in his quest, his work here is nearly done.
There's a creak and a rumble looming just ahead, a significant movement as we finally reach the portcullis that has dragged us here. On our arrival the door begins to open. Our journey has

reached a crossroads and as the door begins to move we notice the dark water glimmering in reflection on the door's huge gothic hinges. We see just how deep and dark we are in, we see just how low we have sunk, just how far we have fallen.

Then the music becomes louder. The crackling of the turntable continues, but somehow the actual music has become more prominent, more over powering. We pause for just a second to listen. We know this song so well, we know every word and every note. Time freezes for just a second as the penny drops and we identify the notes that are following us along the tunnel. It is our love song. The song that was hers and ours, the song that we fell in love too, the song that has ripped us apart every time we have heard it since she discarded us.

The creaking continues as the door slowly and effortlessly opens, inviting us to step inside. We pause for a second, gently putting our hand onto the door frame to stop the momentum of the black stream that has carried us this far. Once again, we feel a flurry on our heel and we look down just in time to see a rat brush past our ankle bone and then ahead through the frame into pitch black. We cannot tell whether it is the same rat that ran past us earlier, but we know that rats' deserting anything is not a good sign, there is that age old saying about rats and a sinking ship!

Something bad is coming behind us and there could be something even worse ahead. We have no choice but to follow the rabid creature through the castle door, following the notorious deserter.

We walk through the door, as the loud shrill of a triumphant bellow echo all around us. The sound of the bull knowing his mission is complete. Such a victorious cry full of passion and pride. He was given a job and he has succeeded whilst we have failed. He lets out another little howl then silence. We stand stock still just the other side of the door gathering our composure, then the atmosphere takes a new direction. Once again, we hear the hooves that have followed us on this last part of our decline, only this time they are retreating. The bull is leaving to go and bring someone else. We have gone through the door; his job is done. We are finished, defeated, he has won and has a new game to take our place. Fresh meat to bring to wherever we are going.

We try to quickly gather our composure; the noise vibrating down the corridor means we are oblivious to the fact the water beneath our feet has quickly reached a new high of shin level. We are going down deeper metaphorically and also physically. We do not seem to notice either, our sole aim is to try and focus on where we are as our eyes strain to become accustomed to the pitch black. There is no light, no windows, nothing. Total darkness, as the sloshing around our shins starts to sound more like a ripple than a splash because of the depth we are in, we begin to feel that we are being watched once more.

We move forward, hands and arms outstretched like a mummy in a Scooby doo cartoon, both desperate to feel something familiar in front of us, but also terrified to reach out and grab a monster. Our heart is pounding so loud that we are sure we can hear it even above the noise of the water. Every hair on our body is standing to attention, like soldiers lined up and ready to go to war against an unknown army.

We walk for what seems like minutes but is actually just a few seconds, till the worry makes us stop. There is definitely something else here. Coming to a standstill, we tilt our head from side to side desperately trying to hear a familiar noise or at least recognise a sound from the long lost outside world. Nothing. No deep strains of breath or cries from the bull that has followed us all our life. He has served his purpose and is now long gone and watching somebody else. Even the love song has begun to fade along with the Bull's hoof steps, it's as if the pain hearing those notes has caused was all linked and controlled by him.

This new guest is something completely different, more intense, more sinister and more evil. The presence that we are feeling now is darkness itself, wicked beyond belief and of a greater threat that the Bull that has haunted us for so long.

Although we feel another, something so close, our ears tell us that we are alone.

Without our brain realising we are doing it, our body begins to turn. Slowly and awkwardly like a huge liner turning to leave dock we begin to move three hundred and sixty degrees, our eyes flicking left to right, left to right, left to right, frantically looking for something we recognise, even if we could just make out a shape.

We see nothing, hear nothing and feel nothing. Our senses are numbed by the stillness. We are surrounded by nothing but darkness.

We are just about complete our circle though, when something does eventually catch our eye. Something off to our left about fifteen yards away, something big and bulky, something for us to aim for. We begin to move in that direction, wading through water that is now above our knees. It's as if we are walking in slow motion, striding out across the moon as we put all our concentration into reaching the only object we can see.

The floor has become uneven now, we hadn't noticed before because we were concentrating on using our eyes. Earlier it was smooth, like walking on concrete, but now it seems the deeper the water the more unsteady our tread. Stones and small boulders litter the pathway to the object, making it even more difficult to walk and, although it may be our imagination, the temperature of the water seems to of risen.

We stumble just five yards away from the object, still unable to work out exactly what the goal we are striving for actually is. We stretch our fingers out trying to grab something to keep us afloat, even now trying to save our self, even though we know we are far too late.

The opening and closing becomes more manic, scissor like, grabbing out at the stagnant air all around us, but there is nothing there, we are alone.

We go down, falling like a felled antelope and with the same grace. The splash fills the room with the force of a waterfall as we are submerged into the bitter fluid that up until now had only drowned below our knees. Our mouth fills with the taste of something rotten, rotten and hot as we realise once again that the temperature of the water has risen. The heat and the repulsive taste makes us gag whilst under and bile floats up our nostrils as it exits from our mouth into the mass that has totally engulfed us, burning our airwaves and making us splutter and swallow.

We are panicking and scared, this is literally an existence in hell. We push our self up with all of our might, propelling our body out of the dark lake and through the yellow pool of bile floating on the surface before it moves away with the tide. Gasping for air to breath and to clear the poison from our nostrils, we struggle for dear life.

We've lost our bearings completely and as we manage to stand, gathering our nerves we see the water is now up to waist level and rising, but having moved in the current too, the object of our desire is there now right in front of us. We clamber towards it, desperate for something to cling too.

We rub our eyes that are stinging beyond belief from the putrid sewage, in order to clear our vision and also because we cannot believe what we are seeing.

Right in front of us there is a huge crimson metallic throne. Deep in colour and huge in size, there is a dull sound echoing deep from the seat itself, a low dulcet tone like the one that comes from a musical pitching fork.

"Huuuummmmmmm"

Within seconds it becomes monotonous, and almost nauseous. However, the pull of it draws us deeper, like a magnetic homing beacon it drags us nearer to the throne. We are desperate to touch it, taken in by its lure, we have an unnatural need to feel it.

The metallic surface is clear to see, but as we reach out and touch it with our right hand we realise why it is such a dark and deep crimson colour. The huge seat fit for a king is red hot. Glowing hot in fact, that must be why the water all around is also heating up. The throne is the element, the room is the kettle and we are set up to boil.

The burns on our finger tips sting with a bitter and almost unbearable force. A personal attack on us, our body and our mind. Attacks are things that we are beginning to get used to, but this one is self inflicted and that makes the deep surge of pain up our fingers to our wrist even more unforgiving and resentful. So foolish, why did we reach out like that?

The water is getting warmer too, warmer and deeper. Up to our chest and rising in volume and heat, we are being boiled alive as bubbles begin to break through and reach the surface. We are well and truly in too far now, in too deep. In a situation we can't handle and, one it appears we can't get out of alive. Lobsters in the pot.

The heat is getting beyond uncomfortable, as we turn the way we came, desperately looking for a way out. Water splashes up into

our face. Leaving a burning, tingling sensation across our cheeks, just like sun burn the day after a person has been hung out to dry in the mid day sun. We can feel the blood rush to our face, as the vessels fill with warm fluid to try and protect. Our face that once stood so proud and was a window into our soul is now violated. Our exterior is stinging, our pride hurting. How the fuck did we end up in this hell and so worn down and broken?
It's then a huge shiver runs the length of our spine. The shiver in itself gives us a shock, how can we shiver when it's so hot now? So hot that beads of sweat are beginning to form on the top of our head, running like little streams down our skull and creating little waterfalls off our more prominent features. A large one hangs from the end of our nose, but we are too afraid to wipe it off. We are beginning to shut down and collapse inwards. We are too frightened to move.
We are no longer alone.
Our body turns back anti clockwise. Our brain seems to have shut itself off from its conscious self and flicked into an automatic mode, a sixth sense. Our heart tells us to run, but the water stops us moving. Our inner brain has gone into melt down and some kind of self destruct mode, it makes our body continue its pivotal journey back towards the throne, it wants us to face what is there even if it is bad, even if it will lead us to death.
Our brain wants to destroy us. It's now fighting against our better judgment, knowing that the darkness has taken over and inside every inch of us is now fighting a war against our self. We close our eyes and hope they never open again, but our inner brain tells us to stop turning just at the right moment. Just right for facing the being that has joined us down here in this bubbling pan of hell. We steady our self and then open our eyes.
We wish we were alone again, we wish we were already dead, anything to not be here facing him.
Sitting proud and glowing red, a brighter poppy red and hotter than the throne below, is Satan himself. A wicked and sickening smile stretched across his face which is nothing more than a hollow crimson skull. His eyes have nothing behind them, just glowing flames that burn our vision every time we look into them.

He has brought us here. He is the one behind the fall, he is the one that is responsible for our journey down to the depths of despair and he is continuing to drag us further into the abyss.

The water has risen further. Up past our chin, we have to tilt our head back to avoid swallowing it by the gallon. A few mouthfuls have already found their way down our throat, scalding our tonsils and leaving an overpowering taste of salt. Salt that will dry out our organs from the inside as it travels through our body. We are being consumed, eaten alive, devoured, killing our organs one by one. The devil is destroying us from the inside first. We feel our flesh burn. It feels like the skin itself is beginning to peel off our body, but we can't see anything through the steaming water that is glowing red itself now. A deep dark red that gives the impression we are being drowned in our own blood. Everything in our life has hurt, ripped us apart, hut nothing compares to the pain we are feeling now.

The salt reaches our nostrils now, red water flowing into our nose at a pace we just can't avoid. Our every sense being attacked by the harsh and coarse texture of the ruby fluid that is seeping into our body through every orifice. Killing us from the inside out.

We are going under, we have slipped, we have fallen and now we have nothing left.

We look for the door from which we entered but it's gone forever. We are too late; there is nothing but water and a red glow in the darkness. The exit must be there somewhere, but we'll never find it, our once chance of escape is lying under the ruby water like the titanic, although unlike that magnificent vessel, it will never be seen again.

We panic. Once again, our inner brain makes us turn towards the throne and, as we feel the salt enter our eye sockets making our vision blur, we see Satan is laughing. Throwing his head back in deep, hysterical laughter that is just a muffled noise to us now, our ears are too far submerged into the red to hear anything more than a drone through the vibrations.

The flames in his eyes glowing like the lava out of a freshly erupting volcano, he laughs and laughs. He has brought us here. This was his plan all along, to suck us all the way in and all the way down. Just at that point he leans forward, stretching towards us and offers us a bony gloved hand…..

He is the only way out....

We have reached our end, you the reader have reached.....

THE END

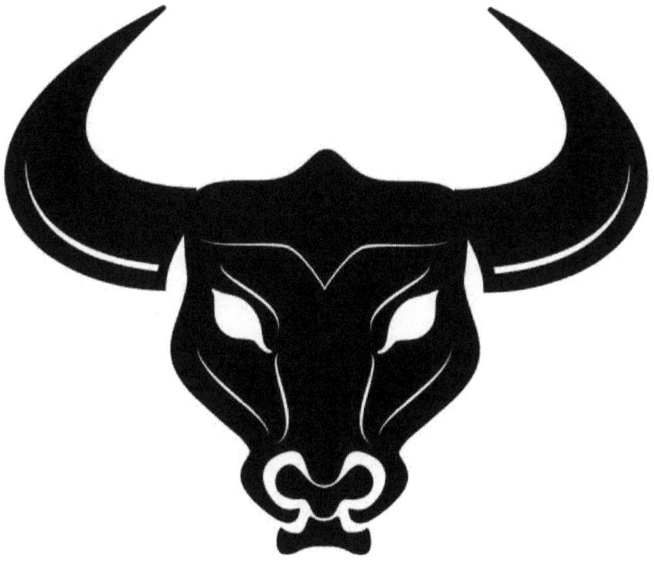